LEGENDS OF THE ANCIENTS

LEGENDS OF THE ANCIENTS

TALES OF THE FEISTY DRUID™ BOOK 8

CANDY CRUM

MICHAEL ANDERLE

L M B P N

DISRUPTIVE IMAGINATION

LMBPN Publishing
PMB 196, 2540 South Maryland Pkwy
Las Vegas, NV 89109

First US edition, June 2020
eBook ISBN: 978-1-64202-966-6
Print ISBN: 978-1-64202-967-3

THE LEGENDS OF THE ANCIENTS TEAM

Thanks to the Beta Readers

James Caplan, Larry Omans, Mary Morris , Kelly O'Donnell,
Nicole Emens

Thanks to our JIT Readers

Daniel Weigert
Dave Hicks
James Caplan
Deb Mader
Diane L. Smith
Dorothy Lloyd
Paul Westman

If we've missed anyone, please let us know!

Editor
The Skyhunter Editing Team

CHAPTER ONE

High above the ship, the bright blue sky held only a few slow-moving thick white clouds. The crashing of the ocean against the ship wrapped around Arryn, who was meditating.

Water continuously splashed her, sitting as she was cross-legged on the bow of the ship. Mariana had been worried about the druid falling off, but Arryn was sure she would be fine. The rail formed a point on the bow, and the wood was thick enough to form a spot perfect for sitting—a spot Arryn gladly took advantage of.

Though Esmerelda was dead and gone, Mariana's job still wasn't done. She and Captain Veren still hunted for other Storm Raiders. Because of this, crossing the sea took longer than usual. Mariana wanted to avoid using magic that could be sensed by another Caller, giving away their pursuit.

While talking to Mariana, Arryn had learned just how rough traveling the seas had become. Much like the bandits invading the Valley, Raiders had taken to the seas, docking wherever they could take advantage of those weaker than them.

Because of everything that had happened in Kemet, Arryn

was in a hurry to get there, but she was also grateful for the extra time. The idea of meeting creatures from another world didn't sit well with her. Men were scary enough, but monsters? *Real* monsters?

Remnant could be terrifying, and they were terrible in their own way, but they were nothing like what Margit had shown her. Remnant couldn't hold a candle to the things she had seen, the things Julianne had shared with Margit.

The long trip not only gave her time to mentally prepare for the journey she would make across the desert, but it also gave her time to work with the bracelet. Except when she needed to sleep, Arryn spent her time checking in with the Temple.

As an ever-growing distance opened between her and everything familiar to her, it was important that she maintain whatever connection she could manage. Keeping in touch with Margit could potentially save their lives. Though Arryn had never met Julianne, it was the master mystic's updates that would more than likely keep them from being some demonic creature's food.

In fact, it was because of Julianne that she had the bracelet. She and her friends had created it in case of an emergency. She had even given one to Amelia, which would allow Arryn to keep in contact with the Arcadian governor to make sure all was well in the Valley.

As much as Arryn loved the forest, she couldn't deny her love for the sea. She could understand the Daoine people better now. Heading south from the Heights in search of the bandits had led to her meeting the most interesting people.

The water dwellers were kind and family-oriented. They showed her how to appreciate the sea. It was beautiful and simple but complicated. Unlike the forest, whose beauty and life—both plant and animal—were on full display, the sea sheltered everything far below. Its true beauty was hidden to anyone on the surface.

But so were the dangers.

The Daoine people were the only ones who could see it for what it was. They could travel far below the surface and discover new life and new dangers. Everyone else was limited to short peeks at what the water had to offer, which only lasted as long as their lung capacity did. The incredible animals, the predators, the prey, and the unique plant life within it were unlike anything Arryn had seen.

The druid focused on the sky, allowing the sunlight and splash of the seawater to calm her and distract her from the stickiness of her skin. She wasn't used to using oils to protect herself from the sun, and the olive- and coconut-oil mixture smelled nice but made her feel dirty.

"Having any luck?" Cathillian asked. He was leaning against the rail to her left.

Arryn grinned, her eyes still shut as she sat with her palms open and facing upward. "I was until you came over here."

Her mental magic had grown enough in the past few days that she was able to sense his amusement. "I'm that distracting, huh?"

She almost snorted. "You are when you won't shut that mouth of yours."

He leaned over and placed his mouth next to her ear. "What about this? Is this distracting?" His voice was low, almost a whisper, and had a heated tone.

She knew he couldn't see the smile on her face or her irises turn black with the subtle flick of her wrist. A ribbon of water lifted from the sea and arced over the rail to swat Cathillian on his backside.

"Apparently not," he said with amusement in his voice. He stepped back to his original position. "Why is it that I lose my mind when you do something as simple as smile a certain way, but I can't distract you as easily?"

Her eyes opened as she turned to him and smiled again. "Oh, I'm easily distracted. In fact, I'd say I'm far worse than you.

However, this is important, and it could potentially save our lives. I don't want to mess it up."

He nodded and laughed. "Well, if you *are* as easily distracted as I am, I'm glad you're more responsible than me."

"I've stayed connected to Margit, but reaching Amelia has proven to be somewhat of a pain in my ass. But don't worry, I'll get it."

Meditation came easily in such peaceful conditions, but reaching Amelia had been very difficult because the distance was much greater.

"Maybe you're going about it all wrong," Cathillian said. "Mental magic is much different than the other two forms. I don't pretend to know anything more about it than that, but even as different as it is, I assume it works just like any other form. Emotions play a part. Instead of sitting here focusing yourself into a headache, focus on your fear. I know the journey ahead of us scares you. Think about that. There might be a time when the worst could happen and you have to call Amelia for help."

A chill ran down her spine. He was right. She was terrified, and she hadn't admitted it to herself. While she knew it was true, it was one thing to say, "I'm afraid," and quite another to immerse herself in the dreaded emotion, allowing it to take her over in the hope that it might break her down and rebuild her stronger.

Using anger to fuel magic was easy, but using fear meant allowing herself to go to dark mental places. She didn't like to do that if she could help it.

Unfortunately for her, it seemed she had no other choice because simple concentration hadn't worked, and this was important.

She nodded and closed her eyes, once again focusing on the tranquility around her. Cathillian didn't say another word as she stilled. Since meeting Corrine, Arryn's biggest motivation had been the young girl. That was who she focused on now.

She thought about getting to Kemet and facing down a

monster she had no idea how to kill, and she wondered if human weapons would work against such a creature. She began to think about the lack of trees in the desert and where the young girl would hide.

Her breath hitched, and she was flooded with guilt for bringing her. Arryn thought of every scenario that could happen, everything that could go wrong and could get Corrine hurt. There were many, so it didn't take much.

Anxiety took her over, and she used it to reach out. First, the only mental link she could touch was the one she had with Margit, but she continued to push, knowing Corrine's life might one day depend on it. Soon, she felt the brush of a familiar mind.

Amelia? Arryn asked telepathically.

Arryn? You've come a long way with your mental magic, haven't you?

The druid sighed, her shoulders slumping as relief rushed through her. *I didn't think I'd be able to do this. We're on a ship in the middle of the sea.*

She could feel Amelia's amusement. *That's quite a distance. You have been practicing. I take it this means you have a bracelet?*

I do. Those were Margit's orders, but I can't say I'm upset about it. After what she showed me, I'm grateful for it. I've seen what we're in for, and it's scary as hell.

Though she didn't mean to, once they were mentioned, Amelia thought of several different kinds of monsters, forcing Arryn to see them through the link.

Sorry about that. I can feel you cringe through the link, Amelia said. *It's hard not to think about them when they're mentioned. Do you know the condition of Kemet? Have you heard anything?*

No. So far, we haven't come across any other Kemetians. I suppose that will change once we reach land. Arryn inhaled deeply, the scent of the sea calming her. The chills brought on by her anxiety and fear of what they faced began to recede.

Now that I have you, I wanted to update you, Arryn continued.

The bandits have been dealt with. Their leader was killed, and so were most of their men, although some fled. I don't think you'll see much more out of them, especially now that they know we're more than capable of hunting them down and putting a stop to their antics.

Relief flooded the link. *I'm very happy to hear that. I assume you've updated Margit. I'll inform the city and send messengers across the Valley. You have no idea how much comfort this will bring the people.*

Yep. Margit knows, and she promised to send word to Craigston. You should be able to order crystals again without fear of the rearicks being injured.

Arryn felt a rush of gratitude and relief from Amelia. *You've done so much for us, enough that we will never be able to repay you.*

The druid smiled. *You don't have to repay me for anything. No one does. My entire childhood, and up until the last year, I obsessed over the need to help Arcadians get their lives back. I wanted to right the wrongs committed by Adrien. It took a while, and even though I didn't get to stop him myself, I was able to help stop his psychotic daughter and find a path where I could help even more people. This was what I was meant to do, and it's an honor to do it.*

Well, we're all grateful anyway. You and Hannah are the best things to have come out of this city. Please let me know if there is ever anything I can do for you, Amelia replied.

Arryn thought for a moment. *Actually, there is one thing. It would mean a lot to me if you would check on my father from time to time. A messenger would be just fine if you can't get away. I just need to know everyone there is okay. Without being able to send Echo back and forth, and with no one in the forest knowing how to use mental magic, this will be the only way for me to find out how he and everyone else are doing.*

Absolutely. I'll send a messenger this afternoon. Next week, I'll make sure to go myself. We can alternate, and I will talk to Julianne. There might be a way for me to mentally connect to your father when I'm there and be a bridge to link the two of you.

Arryn was excited about possibly being able to talk to her father directly during Amelia's visits. That would be amazing. It would be great to get updates about him and everyone else in the forest, but it was not possible to speak to him herself.

Thank you! That would be...

Arryn was pulled away from Amelia when she heard screams. Her eyes snapped open, but she could feel Amelia's mind brushing against hers with urgency. *We have a situation here,* Arryn sent. Reconnecting was easier with Amelia reaching for her at the same time. *Everyone is fine, but there are a lot of bodies in the water. I'll check in later.*

Stay safe, Amelia sent before the link was broken.

CHAPTER TWO

Arryn stood on the rail and looked at the water. Floating pieces of wood held the living on the surface, people who were badly sunburned and waving the ship down. The disturbing part was the nearly fifty floating bodies, some of which had been torn to bits and scattered about.

"What the hell happened?" Cathillian asked, his fists clenching as anger scrunched his expression.

"Raiders," Storm Caller Mariana said from behind them.

Arryn's nostrils flared as she shook her head. "Doesn't matter. We need to get those people on the ship."

Her eyes flashed as she widened her stance on the rail and prepared to call her magic. Mariana grabbed her ankle. The druid looked down at the Caller, who shook her head. "We can lower boats and collect them. I can't see or sense a ship, but if we run into them, we might need your magic. It would be best if you didn't use it to retrieve them since I know you'll expend more energy to heal them after. Those people will be fine with boats. Conserve your strength."

With a sigh, Arryn nodded. "Fine. But they need to be healed while you're lowering the boats."

"On it!"

A dark-skinned blur rushed past her, jumped over the rail, and executed a perfect dive into the water. In seconds, Corrine's head popped above the surface, and she swam toward the survivors.

"There is *no* stopping her," Cathillian said.

Arryn smiled. "No, there really isn't."

Arryn dove in as well and as she rose to the surface, she propelled herself through the water. She had learned the trick from the Daoine, though she wasn't that good at it. Corrine had apparently learned as well because she beat Arryn to the first survivor.

"Thank you, little one," a man said.

Corrine smiled as she laid one of her hands on the side of his face. In seconds, the sunburn lightened, his skin began to look healthier, and his lips became plumper as the cracks disappeared. The life came back into his eyes, and he thanked her again.

"Try not to use too much at once," Arryn said. "We have quite a few people to heal."

Corrine nodded. "I know. We could have a fight if the Raiders come back, too. I'll be careful."

Arryn gave a curt nod before leaving the girl to do what she did best. The Arcadian druid came to the first survivor after pushing several dead bodies out of the way. A quick pulse check told her he barely clung to life, and his skin was blistered from the hot sun.

"Everything's going to be okay," she said as she laid her hand on his shoulder.

Healing energy passed through her hand into the man's weakened body. He jerked and then groaned as the blistered and painful sun-induced injuries to his ebony skin healed, then he opened his eyes.

"Thank you," he said in a forced whisper.

"Just rest. I didn't heal you completely, I just took away the worst of your injuries. Once we get you on the boat, we'll get you some fresh water, okay?" Arryn smiled.

His eyes closed again, but his hand weakly squeezed hers in response. She felt terrible that she couldn't heal him more, but there were so many people in the water, she couldn't use it all on a single person.

She and Corrine moved from person to person as the smaller boats came to pick up survivors. Cathillian sat in one of the boats, pulling people in and giving them another quick round of healing.

It took quite a while to get everyone on the ship, but once onboard, Arryn and her crew were able to get everyone situated and give them fresh food and water.

Dozens of bodies lay in pieces in the water, destroyed in the battle or ripped apart by marine wildlife. Those who survived had been incredibly lucky to not end up as shark bait with all the blood and fresh meat in the water. Had a few more hours passed, they would have all been goners.

Mariana was able to get answers from those who weren't as badly injured, but most fell asleep soon after eating. Arryn couldn't imagine how exhausted they must have been, even after having healing energy pushed through them.

The druid finished bandaging the superficial wounds of a sleeping woman and returned to the bow of the ship. "One of the crew told me a few minutes ago that you managed to find out what happened?"

Mariana nodded. "It was another Storm Ship. There are a few stragglers out there, and they feed on smaller ships. They overtake them, take anything they need or want—including food and supplies—and then destroy the ship. This one was no different, except they left people alive after destroying it. That's new and even crueler than usual, but I'm not surprised."

Arryn shook her head. "The world will never be short of people who surprise us with the level of evil in their hearts." The

Arcadian druid sighed heavily, a worried expression on her beautiful face. "Look…"

The Storm Caller smiled. "I know. Don't worry about us. We'll be fine."

"I'm sorry we can't help you with this one. Bast and Cleo came to the Dark Forest so long ago asking for help, and their home was in danger back then. We've had a lot of things happen since. I haven't spoken to them about it, but I know it's been on their mind."

"You worry you might be too late."

Arryn looked into the Caller's compassionate eyes. "Yes. The things attacking them…they're not from our world. I don't know what they are, but they're scary as hell, and they've been there for a while. I'm terrified their homeland has already been destroyed and their family is dead."

"We knew that was a risk when we came to find you," Cleo said from behind Arryn.

Arryn turned to see Cleo's dark skin glistening in the sun. Half her hair was in thin, uniform box braids. The other half was sectioned into naturally shiny black poofs. It was obvious she and Bast had been in the middle of re-braiding Cleo's hair when the excitement had broken out.

"I'm sorry. I didn't realize you were standing there," Arryn said. "I used a lot of energy, so my senses aren't what they usually are."

Cleo waved a hand. Between her and her sister, Cleo was calmer and more calculated. She wasn't *cold*, but she was realistic and serious most of the time. Both women had great senses of humor, but Bast was the more carefree of the two of them.

The woman took a step forward. "I came up here to check on you and overheard the conversation. Don't worry about Kemet like that. Our mother raised us to be strong. Our people might have backward ways of thinking with tradition sometimes trumping common sense, but she raised us to overcome all that.

It was our duty to come and find you, no matter the cost. When you get there, you'll understand why we are the way we are and why we risked everything to find you. If Jadid still stands, we'll fight for it. If it doesn't, we'll avenge it."

Arryn forced a smile, but she couldn't shake her worry. "I realize it's not my place to worry about your city, but I can't help it. You came to me for aid, and you helped me *several* times. I'm worried about arriving and finding only sand and bone where your people used to be."

Cleo gave a soft smile. "If the city has fallen, it *will* rise again. Don't you worry about that."

A look of confusion crossed Arryn's face. "What do you mean?"

"The people will survive. You know me; I'm pragmatic. I look at the situation in front of me, and I calculate what needs to be done to make a goal achievable. My mother is the same way, but she's also optimistic like Bast. She sent us to you out of hope, but the side of her that sees reality compelled her to put plans in place that would save the city if the worst were to happen. Trust me, if Jadid is gone, the people aren't. At least, not all of them."

Bast wandered up, stretching her arms. "Besides, had we returned to Kemet without helping you save your people and the others we met on the way, do you know what our mother would have done to us?"

Arryn laughed. "If your mom's anything like Elysia, you probably would have been in for quite a beating."

Bast nodded. "Exactly. I'd sooner go back and live with the strange water-dwelling Daoine people than return to Kemet and tell her we left a bunch of hurting people behind us to rush home to save our own. Of course, if we'd done that, I wouldn't have met the Daoine, but you know what I mean. Anyway, Kemetians are tough, but we aren't afraid to ask for help when we need it."

"Make no mistake," Cleo continued. "Kemet is in grave danger, but the people are much different than those you're used to from Arcadia. They won't just run around screaming until they die. Whatever those bastards are, this is a fight they won't soon forget. Kemetians won't go down without fighting. Even if they get to a point where it seems defeat is unavoidable, our mother will *not* fail."

Mariana clapped Arryn on the back. "See? Leave the worrying to them. Since they don't seem afraid of the fate they might meet, you shouldn't be either. It'll only distract you. You're one of the strongest people I've ever met, but your heart is so big that it gets in the way of your brain sometimes."

That made a lot of sense to Arryn. She'd always been a thinker, and thinking sometimes got her into trouble. Most of the time, her will carried her through, but like anyone, there were times when she let doubt consume her. This was one of those moments.

Taking a deep, calming breath, Arryn reassured herself that if the twins weren't scared, she shouldn't be either. She would wait until they arrived to decide how to feel. Even then, she wouldn't have time to think too much about it, not when lives would be at stake.

CHAPTER THREE

Asim made her way down the palace steps to the stone walkway, holding her head high as she moved. Her long red royal robes flowed behind her as she strode toward the gathering of men, women, and children gathered outside.

"Good morning," she said with a smile.

"Good morning, Your Highness," her people greeted her in turn.

Asim looked toward the west for a moment. In the distance, she saw a large group of people walking toward the palace. Clouds and darkness still clung to the sky overhead, but to the east, the sky had begun to turn yellow and orange.

It would have been a beautiful sight, but all she could think of was the danger that lurked far to the south.

Their days were numbered if they didn't do something soon.

Luckily for them, Asim had a plan to ensure the safety of everyone.

"Last night's workers are coming in, and we'll soon replace them," Asim said loudly and proudly. "Each of us has a full belly, and we have set out a beautiful meal for them to eat before sleeping for the day. Our soldiers are guarding our borders to make certain we are safe while we work. These are not the greatest of conditions, but we have made the best of what we have to work with."

Asim was their queen, and as such, every life in Jadid was her responsibility. When they had first appeared several months back, the creatures had been smaller as well as few and far between. Over the last few weeks, however, reports coming from the south said they were much larger.

Not many people risked venturing too close to the portal anymore, so it was hard to get reports, but she understood.

For the most part, the attacks happened in smaller villages, but they had increased in frequency. Because of that, plans had been put in place to ensure the safety of everyone inside the royal city as well as the people scattered throughout Kemet.

Unfortunately, that required secrecy. If anyone with a dark heart were to learn of the tunnels being built under Jadid and to the north, they could invade and harm those under her care. She hated to do it, but increasing security was incredibly important.

Before closing the gates, Asim had invited all those who lived outside the city. They had all been encouraged to gather their supplies and crops and move inside the walls. Asim wanted everyone in her kingdom taken care of. Though it had never been done before, Asim had even opened the doors of the palace to the public.

Carefully selected and secured areas of the palace had been converted into temporary housing for those who needed it. Asim had also commissioned homes to be built in neighboring large towns that were safe for those seeking refuge from the south.

Each newcomer in the city was assigned a job, one they had to accept and complete with pride if they were to live for free inside the great city. Within a few weeks, everything fell into a rhythm, and Queen Asim set her plan in motion.

At night, workers moved into the tunnels that Asim and her most skilled and trusted architects had designed. Once the sun began to rise, those inside the palace made enough food to feed themselves as well as the workers returning from their long shift.

After eating, they made their way outside and traded places with the night shifters, Asim among them. Though she was queen, she was a firm believer in hard work and leading people by example. She had raised her children to do the same.

Once the palace beds had been remade and the tables cleared of dishes from Asim's group and re-set with plates full of hot food, it was time to start the day.

"Today, we'll begin creating the maze tunnels. I'll lead the diggers. The rest of you will be reinforcers. As we remove the earth, you will stabilize and harden the walls and ceilings," Asim instructed.

"Your Highness," Abram, one of the night shift diggers, said with a respectful bow of his head.

"Abram, good morning," the queen responded. "Any problems to report?"

He shook his head. "We nearly doubled the progress we made the night before. Things are moving much more smoothly. If we keep working at this rate, we should be finished within a month."

Asim nodded. "Let us hope we *have* a month. We'll focus on the most important parts. The night shift will continue to work on the main tunnel, and we'll work on the false tunnels and creating traps. Thank you for your labor. Please rest well."

Abram and his team bowed deeply before moving toward the food.

Asim sent her team into the tunnels to inspect the work done the night before while she looked over the plans. The underground network would be a fortress once finished. Above ground, soldiers surrounded the city on tall, thick walls they hoped would be enough to keep the monsters at bay.

The top of each wall had an armored walkway, which allowed the guards to move freely around the city if positions needed to be changed. Every smith in Jadid was busy crafting new weapons from scrap metal taken from buildings left over from the ancients in the past capital of Kemet. They stocked the wall as well as stockpiled more to hide inside the tunnels.

If an emergency evacuation were needed, the city would gather at the palace and head into the tunnels. Once everyone was inside, the ground would be closed tight, making the entry invisible to anyone above ground and cutting off any scent left behind. Asim couldn't imagine anything would be able to smell them that far down.

Every family in the city had been assigned a number between one and four that represented which tunnel they went to when the time came. That would decrease the risk of confusion and panic.

The tunnels twisted and turned, intersecting with fake passageways stocked with supplies to make them look real. This would stall any enemy that may find their way in. In those false tunnels were traps meant to kill.

The families' elders had been tasked with memorizing the layout of the tunnel system and teaching their family, going over them every day to ensure no wrong turns would be made.

Every day, they would go to the palace to study one of several copies so they could all be burned when the evacuation was announced. That would prevent any attacker, human or otherwise, from stumbling upon their routes.

Kemetians were extremely detailed in their work and prided themselves on perfection. Anything less was disappointing, and in this case, dangerous. While the city had once been a patriarchal society, Asim's rise to power after the death of her father had changed things, and the quality of work within their borders had gotten better.

Asim had stuck to tradition for some time to soften the transition, forcing her daughters to do the same, even though she had taught them to be strong and powerful women regardless of rules. Soon, it became clear that change was essential. Eventually, women began to serve in the army, nearly doubling its numbers overnight—something that was desperately needed.

Though there were still a lot of things to overcome, Jadid had come to rely on Asim and her style of leadership. It was a new time, and while her ideas were radical within their conservative city, she hadn't failed them yet. They looked at her less like a mere woman and more like their rightful queen, which paved the way for women across their society to pick up tools and learn new trades.

Jadid had been reborn, and they weren't about to let it get destroyed. That was for damn sure.

"How much longer do you think it will be before the princesses' return?" Asim's advisor, Omar, asked.

The queen thought for a moment. "If I know Bast and Cleo, they met with trouble along the way. I have no doubt they succeeded on their journey, and we have to make sure we succeed here."

Omar smiled. "They do often find trouble."

Asim returned the smile. "That they do, but I raised them to be fighters. They found the city of magic, I'm sure of it. Soon, they'll return with an army capable of things we've never dreamed of."

Omar nodded. "When they do, we'll be ready."

CHAPTER FOUR

A light gust of wind blew through the Dark Forest, brushing Christopher's face as he sat cross-legged on the edge of the Kalt River. His hands rested palm-up on his knees, and his eyes were closed as he focused on his breathing. The sun touched his face, warming his entire body.

Since being in the Dark Forest and away from the dark druids, Christopher had spent every day trying to better himself. Each day freedom graced him, and he felt another piece of himself return.

At first, every night was plagued with dark dreams and horrible memories of the life he'd been forced to live for over ten years. Arryn and the others had healed his body of the decade of damage taken from the many poisons he'd been forced to test, but his mind still suffered.

The young mystic Zoe had worked with Elysia to heal his mind of the terrors, and since then, he'd worked to strengthen his body. The stronger he became physically, the more confidence he found. Every day, he remembered more of who he was before his wife died and his daughter was lost to him.

Sitting in the sun today, Christopher felt almost like himself.

Elysia had asked the village leatherworker to create new clothing and armor for him since his body had changed.

His arms, chest, back, and thighs were much thicker now than when he'd first arrived. He'd been terribly thin, with little muscle definition. Now, thanks to his diet and the lifestyle he led in the Dark Forest, combined with the daily training and healing sessions, his body was stronger than it had been before he'd been taken from Arcadia.

In the last few days, Christopher had been thinking about his magic. He'd excelled in warrior training, and like his daughter, he wanted more. Life was far too short, and Arryn had accomplished so much. He was her father, yet it was she who was an inspiration for him. He wanted to learn everything he could to make sure no one he loved was ever harmed again.

The Dark Forest and everyone within it had become his family. They had given so much to him when he had nothing. If he couldn't protect them, what good was he? In his mind, he would be useless.

Every day, Christopher came to the river to meditate and think about the decisions he had in front of him. He had to speak to Nika, Elysia, and the Chieftain since he wanted to be more than an Arcadian in warrior training. If Arryn had become a druid, he wanted to do the same.

He also wanted to be a warrior. A *true* warrior.

That would require knowledge of nature magic, something he'd had little training in. He'd tried, but it hadn't gone well. He felt silly learning alongside the children, even though he loved being around them. They were all so full of life, and they reminded him of the happiness he'd felt when Arryn was so little.

Still, if they continued to allow him the opportunity, he'd train next to the little ones. If a rearick could learn nature magic, it wouldn't be a stretch for him since he already knew physical magic.

Though he'd never been as strong with magic as his late wife, he was very powerful. He was stronger than Arryn had been when she left for Arcadia if the stories Elysia and the Chieftain had told him were true. It seemed she'd grown exponentially in a short period from sheer determination and the need to protect those she loved.

As soon as I get back to the village, I'll do it. I'll speak to them, he thought.

His eyes shot open when he heard a stick snap. As loud as it was, he knew it must have been thick, meaning whatever had broken it wasn't human. No animals within the Dark Forest barrier, aside from Chaos and Zobig, were large enough to make a noise like that.

Christopher's heart skipped with the adrenaline jolt that urged him to stand and run, but he knew something watched him from a hidden corner. If he ran, whatever it was would chase him. He had to be cautious.

Terrified and knowing better than to move his body, Christopher swiveled his eyes to see into the woods across the river where he'd heard the sound echo from. A low growl rumbled, and he heard it even over the sound of the rushing water.

Shit.

He knew that sound. That was no bear or wolf.

Lycanthrope.

The hairs on his neck stood as another growl came from his left. Chills raced through him. Carefully, he stayed as still as possible while moving his eyes to see the creature. A tall black and gray lycanthrope stood on thick, powerful legs, its clawed feet gripping the ground, signaling its readiness to pounce.

Its lips were pulled back in a snarl, and drool dripped from jagged teeth that glistened in the sunlight. The beast's arms were at least as thick as Christopher's now-muscular thighs, and its hands were big enough to grip his head like a human holding a melon.

A loud roar sounded from across the river as a tall brown

lycanthrope stepped out of the woods and stalked to the edge of the water. Christopher slowly rose, careful not to make any jerky movements. Every breath was calm and even though his heart raced.

Today is not the day you die. You've survived worse.

Instinctively, Christopher's hands went to his sides, but he'd left his weapons in the village. He mentally kicked himself but accepted his fate. This fight would challenge him, and a deep and curious part of him welcomed it.

If he couldn't defend himself against two beasts, how could he possibly help protect an entire forest full of druids when the time came? How could he protect Arryn? She'd taken on the Weres, even back when she was weaker than he was right at that moment.

For her...

The black and gray lycanthrope on Christopher's left roared as it charged him. In a move that surprised even him, he charged right back.

Christopher rushed forward, studying the beast's every movement. He saw the lycanthrope's arm flex and knew what it planned to do. As it prepared to slash with its claws, his eyes went black.

His hand flexed as his telekinetic energy gripped the lycanthrope's claws, holding them in place. It roared in anger as Christopher used the creature's bent knee as a step. He jumped and flipped backward, his right foot connecting hard with the beast's chin.

Although he landed unevenly, he recovered by executing a graceful somersault that ended with him in a crouch. Movement to his right caught his attention as he saw the brown lycanthrope leap straight for him from the opposite edge of the river.

The black and gray creature had recovered and was on the run again. Christopher had no idea how much power he had. His body had grown physically, but he hadn't tested his magic. If he used too much without having practiced, he might tire too quickly.

But he couldn't deny the desire he felt to test himself.

The brown lycanthrope jumped onto a rock but slipped into the water, getting wet. It pulled itself onto the shore, its rage evident in the snarl on its face, and roared at Christopher in an attempt to reclaim its dominance.

He smiled at the wet beast until he caught movement in his peripheral vision. Christopher's arms arced over his chest, then he thrust them outward. The brown lycanthrope was thrown back into the river as he turned to narrowly avoid a swipe from the black and gray one.

He tumbled out of the way, came to a stop several feet behind the beast, and got to his feet, then ran forward, planting his foot on a large rock that allowed him to jump high into the air. His hands landed flat on the lycanthrope's shoulders, and he pushed himself upward. His vertical momentum, paired with his strength, lifted him high enough to wrap his thick legs around the beast's neck.

Inertia propelled him forward to throw it off-balance. The lycanthrope grabbed Christopher's thighs as it fell, and its claws pierced deep as he tucked his upper body to hit the ground on his shoulders and upper back. With the built-up momentum as the rest of his body followed, he used his legs to pull the lycanthrope the rest of the way over.

The beast landed hard on its back, its claws still buried in Christopher's leg. The would-be druid's eyes changed again as he whipped his hand to the side, using telekinetic energy to throw the lycanthrope several feet away. Blood rushed out as the beast's claws were torn from his thighs and pain radiated through his body, but he wasn't going to give up.

Grabbing a rock a little larger than his hand, Christopher channeled power through it as he squeezed in a much smaller version of something he'd once seen the twins do. Chunks broke away to form a razor-sharp arrowhead-like tip.

As the lycanthrope roared in rage and charged, Christopher looked the beast in the eyes and lifted his right hand, the rock lying flat in his palm. With a flick of his left wrist, the rock shot forward, piercing the creature directly between the eyes to come out the back of its skull.

A loud roar from the edge of the river caught his attention. The brown lycanthrope had triumphed over the current and was about to climb out.

"Not today," Christopher said.

He cried out as he thrust his hands forward, another blast of energy sending it deeper into the water as he forced himself to remain on his feet.

The lycanthrope struggled to sink its claws into the riverbed for traction as Christopher limped toward the water. He wasn't finished yet, but he couldn't stand for much longer. The only chance he had was to fight in the water.

As the beast struggled, Christopher placed a cautious foot on the surface, and the rushing water froze as he focused his energy. Whips of water reached out, wrapping around his legs and waist before freezing to hold him steady.

He risked a step and then another. The ice bent and moved with him under his control, acting as braces as they carried him across the surface. He was no more than ten feet away from his target when it finally found its footing.

"Today is *not* the day I die." Christopher repeated his thought from earlier as the lycanthrope prepared to leap.

His hands rose at his sides, and whips of water and shards of ice lifted from the river. The creature gave an ear-piercing, angry roar, its arms outstretched and mouth wide as it prepared to take down its prey.

But Christopher wasn't to be messed with, something he learned better every day.

His opponent finally leapt, but Christopher was ready. As he flexed his right hand, the whips struck out and held the beast in the air when they froze. It began to snap at its bonds, struggling to free itself and howling in pain as they tightened.

Without hesitation, Christopher flexed his other hand, and ice crystals whistled through the air before tearing through the creature and ending its life. The moment it was over, Christopher exhaled heavily. The triumph hit him hard. Though he hadn't planned to die and had been determined to do quite the opposite, it hadn't been a guarantee. Because he hadn't tested himself magically in so long, he hadn't been certain he would make it through.

Weakened by blood loss and magic use, Christopher slowly turned on the surface of the water and made his way back to land. As the ice bracing him melted and fell to the rocky shore as water, he took a single step, stumbled, and dropped to his hands and knees.

Though pain radiated through him, he began to laugh as he lay on his side and rolled to his back. His survival and exhaustion left him slightly delirious. He couldn't believe how well he'd done, and he truly believed he had Arryn to thank for it. Had it not been for her, he would not have trained so hard.

Another loud shift in the rocks halted his laughter as his senses went on the alert again. Rock crunched around him as an angry black lycanthrope charged on a trajectory that ended with Christopher.

The older man's eyes flashed black once again, and he flexed his entire body. A shield exploded around him as a storm cloud grew out of nothingness overhead. A bright flash blinded Christopher a second before a loud shriek ripped through the sky.

Thunder cracked overhead loudly enough to shake the ground and force Christopher to cover his ears. He opened his eyes to see a limp, lifeless lycanthrope suspended in the air with vines. Smoke rolled off its bare skin, all the fur having burned away.

The vines casually flicked the beast away, and Christopher rolled over to look behind him, his ears ringing. The darkness of the clouds began to fade as he laid eyes on the Chieftain standing at the edge of the forest.

"Meditation peaceful today?" the druid asked.

Christopher smiled. "Very. Care to have a go?"

The Chieftain stepped onto the rocky shore and walked over to the black and gray lycanthrope Christopher had killed with the jagged shard to poke it with his staff. "It looks like you had enough meditation for both of us."

Christopher snorted before flopping back down. "Before I get too comfy lying here and bleeding to death, are there any more around? That last one was a surprise."

There was a pause as he heard the older man walk across the rocks toward him. "No, no more. Just the three. You'd know that if you trained more in nature magic."

"Yeah, I've been meaning to talk to you about that," Christopher said as the Chieftain sat next to him.

"And I'd love to discuss it, but first, you need to be healed. I can sense the infection growing in you already. Their claws are vicious in both the initial attack and afterward. They are filthy creatures, and infections take root quickly. Also, I believe your femoral artery was nicked. I sense a lot of blood loss in that right leg."

Christopher nodded and grinned, though it was interrupted by his face scrunching as he fought the pain. "By all means. Let's sit and talk about it for a while."

The Chieftain laughed at the sarcasm. "That apple of yours certainly didn't fall far from that tree. Your expressions are nearly the same when you give me a hard time."

He placed his hand on Christopher's shoulder, and the old man's jade-colored eyes lit up neon green. Heat rushed through

Christopher, and he could feel his energy return as the wounds closed.

"I miss her," he said. "I feel like I just got her back, and now she's gone again. Well, she's been gone for a while now, but you know what I mean."

Alexander nodded. "I do as well. Life isn't the same without her sarcasm. Plus, I rather enjoy how rough she is on Cathillian. He needs it. He's too much like me."

Christopher laughed. "I agree wholeheartedly. Seems to skip a generation. Elysia is beautiful and funny, but she's not the childish smartasses you and your grandson seem to be. No offense."

The older man shrugged. "I take that as a compliment. Now, about this nature magic. While I was watching…"

"I'm sorry, what? *Watching?*" Christopher asked, shock crossing his face. "Did you say you were watching?"

A large smile graced the Chieftain's face as he lifted his hand, the tips of his thumb and forefinger only a half-inch apart. "Just a little."

Christopher's eyes closed, and he sighed as his head fell back.

"Hey, you'd know that *too* if you trained more in nature magic. You'd be aware of all living things around you. Well, aside from the Mad. Those beasts aren't animal or man."

"I can't say I didn't want to test myself. I was curious to see what I could do, and it wasn't like running was an option. What if I'd died? Anyone ever tell you that you're kind of a dick when you're being sneaky?"

The Chieftain winked. "I *have* been told that a time or two, now that you mention it. Must be true!" He laughed, and Christopher rolled his eyes and smiled. "If I'm honest, I wanted to test you, too. I came to find you after talking to Elysia. I sensed the beasts approaching, and I hurried here with Zobig. When I found you…"

The Chieftain stared deep into Christopher's eyes, studying him.

"What?" Christopher asked.

"I'm no mystic, but I sensed something in you—strength. I was curious. You clearly saw two of them. I could sense the adrenaline coursing through you, yet you stayed still. Not out of fear, since your breathing was surprisingly steady. You seemed very much like a calculating warrior. I was very curious to see what you would do. Had I believed you to be in danger, I would have stepped in."

"I guess I was dead meat on the last one then, huh?"

"Not hardly. I think you could have taken that one, too, but I didn't see a point in forcing you to do so. You were damaged and had proven what you were capable of. I had my answer," the Chieftain said.

"What was that?"

"Elysia said you've been asking a lot of questions. She said you've been asking about advanced training and the qualifications required of a warrior of the Dark Forest. She said she got the impression you wanted more than to just be a guest here. Was she correct?"

Christopher sighed in relief. He hadn't realized he'd been so obvious about it, but he'd wanted it badly. Apparently he'd acted like a child, hinting at something he wanted to do but was afraid to ask for.

He nodded. "I wasn't sure how to ask. I was afraid you wouldn't think I was ready. But yes, I want to learn nature magic, and I want to train to be a warrior."

"Done. You start first thing in the morning. You'll come with me and observe the children. After lunch, you and I will train alone in the forest. Oh, and if you thought Nika and Elysia were hard on you..." Alexander laughed.

Christopher snorted. "Well, I'm not surprised. They're the best."

"They will teach you to be no less than your best as well. Welcome home. Let's get you back before everyone thinks I was drunk and got lost in the woods."

"Has that ever happened?"

The old man rolled his eyes. "Ya have too much sweet wine and wander off *one time*, and no one ever lets you hear the end of it."

Christopher stood as he shook his head. "Yeah, you and Cathillian were *definitely* cut from the same cloth."

CHAPTER FIVE

A rryn stepped away from the injured to check on Mariana as she guided the ship toward land. Arryn could sense the shore approaching fast, and she was excited to see it. What would it look like? Would it all be desert? The twins had told her what a desert was, but it still boggled her mind. Would there be a town? Surely, there would be some form of civilization.

She had so many questions!

Her belly growled as she thought of going to an inn or bar to get something filling to eat. She had no idea what hunting in the desert would be like, but she knew what hunting on a desolate mountain was like, which was *horrible.*

"So, uh, I see land," Arryn said, another growl ripping through her belly.

Mariana nodded and chuckled. "Yep. That's what that big green and brown chunk of dirt over there is."

"Is there food where you're taking us? I'm starving, and I don't want fish."

She nodded. "Oh, yes. This port has excellent food. We had to stop there a while back on one of our many trips through these waters, searching for Raider ships."

That brought a smile to Arryn's face. "Good. I was afraid I might have to resort to eating Cathillian."

Mariana laughed, and Arryn turned at a very distinct clearing of a throat.

Cathillian stood there, hands on hips. "Excuse me? There are plenty of fish in the sea—"

"I'd *still* choose you," Arryn said in a mock-innocent tone, rubbing her belly as she fluttered her eyelashes. Within seconds, she burst into laughter. "Relax. She said there's food, so you're safe...*for now*." She winked.

"Did someone say food?" Bast asked. Cleo was not far behind her.

Arryn nodded. "Seems we might be able to treat ourselves when we get to shore." She looked at Mariana. "Still, this feels wrong. I wish we could go with you. I want to help you track those ships down—especially this one." Her eyes drifted to the wounded. "This seems...unfinished. Unsettled. I don't like it."

The Storm Caller turned toward Arryn and placed a hand on her shoulder. "On the beach during that fight, I told you if that ship came along, I had to go. I told you I couldn't let them go. My fight was with them, but I wanted to help you until I couldn't any longer."

Arryn nodded again. "Still feels wrong, even if I know there's a job to do."

"You're in the same position now that I was then. You helped get all these people out of the water and weakened yourself to heal them. While some still suffer, they won't *die*, and that's all because of you and your friends. You have a job of your own to do, and you need to go. Most important, you need to not feel bad about it. If you finish in Kemet, and you want to come along, you're always welcome on my ship."

"I might just take you up on that," Arryn said, smiling. "Unless someone else needs us along the way."

Cleo came closer. "Hey! Now that we're closer, I can see the outline of the town. That's the same place we came through. It's not a direct shot from the great city, but it's usually pretty busy. We knew there would be a better chance of hitching a ride."

"How many ports are around here?" Arryn asked.

Cleo looked at her incredulously. "I'm a desert dweller, you're a forest dweller, and she more or less lives on the water. Who here do you think is the expert?"

Arryn snorted and laughed. "Fair point. I just assumed you knew the area since you came through before. Oh, and because *you live here.* But I suppose there were several places you could have gotten a ride across."

"Also a fair point. That being said, *steak.*" Cleo audibly sighed. "They have *amazing* steak at one of the inns. Kind of like some of those places in the Valley, but a lot bigger. There are also half-naked ladies, so not all bad."

"Uh, what?" Cathillian and Samuel both said. "Half-naked what?" Cathillian followed up.

Arryn laughed and rolled her eyes. "You're ridiculous."

After eating seafood for nearly two weeks, Arryn and the others were ready to have red meat again. They often ate fresh fish from the river in the Dark Forest, but never more than once or twice a week, and never twice in a row.

Arryn hoped they could find somewhere other than a tavern with scantily clad women, though. Not that she gave a damn, but taking Corrine in there was a different story.

Though the temptation was there to rush the trip so she could find *anywhere* with food, Arryn refrained from using magic to hurry the ship along. Mariana preferred not to, and the druid didn't want to disobey her.

The Caller could sense the use of nature magic, so she understood Mariana's need to be elusive in case they got close to the Raider ship. Arryn didn't want to ruin the woman's chances of finding them.

She and her group stood silently at the rail of the ship, watching the town grow larger the closer they came. While Arryn didn't mind being on the water, she preferred land. Still, she had to admit she wouldn't mind going back one day to visit the Daoine people and play at the beach.

Arryn saw rows of ships as they moved closer to the port. The docks were at least a quarter-mile away, but when she saw families playing on a wide-open beach in front of the town, she thought it was wise placement, whether that had been done on purpose or not.

The families were far more likely to be safe in a wide-open area in front of a busy town than in the more secluded area where the ships docked.

"This is as close as we can get. We don't plan to stay. Give us a moment, and we'll lower the boats for you and your animals. Unfortunately, we're not equipped for unloading horses, so they'll have to swim," the captain said as he wandered up behind them.

Cathillian nodded. "It's not far. These horses love the water, and we'll be with them, so it'll be fine."

Corrine was the first to turn, a smile on her face. "I'm good, thanks!" she said just before jumping over the railing.

Cathillian shook his head. "That girl is feral, I swear."

Arryn laughed. "Yeah, well, she kinda came to us like that, and I'm glad she still has some of it. I hope she never loses her wild spirit." She turned to Captain Veren. "I'll swim to shore. These guys can go with the familiars."

Mariana laughed and pointed. "That's probably for the best, judging by the ripple I see shooting under the water toward the beach. She's already almost on land."

Arryn felt a rough *thump* on her leg and looked down to see a large snow rabbit sitting there. She opened her senses and felt his annoyance.

"Ran off and left you, did she, Whiskers McFluffbutt?" She reached down and picked him up. "Don't worry. I don't think she understands yet what's happening between you two. She still thinks the wolf pup is the one."

She felt a sharp intake of breath from the oversized rabbit before it huffed out a sigh. Pulling him up to her face, she gave his head a little kiss before handing him to Cathillian.

"I'm going after Rin. You guys can take the boats. Please bring my weapons. I don't want them in saltwater again."

Before Cathillian could respond, Arryn dove over the edge, her eyes flashing black as she sliced through the water. She'd learned a thing or two from the Daoine people, but nothing like Corrine. The girl was a fast learner, and Arryn wondered if it was a combination of her age and her stubbornness.

She had no doubt the girl had already reached land, so Arryn needed to get there as quickly as possible. Corrine was strong, but that didn't mean she should be left alone.

Allowing her power to surround her, she propelled herself through the water. It was sloppy and not as fast as Corrine had been, but it worked. She came up for air a few times on the way to shore, not bothering with an air bubble. When she got there, Corrine stood at the water's edge, arms crossed in an impatient pose.

"You're slow," she said, a smile on her face.

Arryn rose to her feet and walked onto the sand. She flicked both hands to the side, and all the excess water pulled away from her body and fell. "You had a head start. No fair!"

"Mmhmm. I'm sure that was it."

Arryn laughed and shook her head. "When it comes to magic, I've learned there are things I'm good at and things I'm not. The water stuff? Definitely not. I can do it, but you're a lot better at it than I am. I have a feeling that's going to happen often, but I'll still be able to kick your butt, so don't get cocky."

Corrine laughed and hugged Arryn. "I love you."

Arryn hugged the little girl tightly. "I love you, too." When she looked toward the ship, she saw two boats being lowered into the water. "Now we have to wait for Cathillian. I might be slower than you, but he's the slowest of all."

Corrine giggled.

"Oh, and what do we have here?"

Arryn groaned as she slowly turned to see four men standing behind them, weapons drawn. Echo called out overhead, and Arryn waved. "I've got this. It's all good."

The four men laughed, and one of them stepped forward. "That's cute. That your pet birdie?"

Arryn snorted. "'Birdie?' Clearly, you're either blind or dumb as hell. My guess is the latter." She delivered a snarky smile. "And if you'd like to leave my presence with the use of your legs, I'd suggest using them to walk away now."

He laughed again, this time much louder. The men behind him joined in. Arryn saw a fifth man headed toward the water, staff in hand. Her eyes narrowed as she examined it.

"No way," she whispered.

Her eyes flashed white, and she looked into his mind. Just on the surface was a memory of him standing at the bow of a large ship, one she didn't see anywhere around as Captain Veren dropped them off.

In the man's recent memory, she saw black clouds form overhead as the wind picked up. The very staff he held now sat in a cup of water as the Caller used his power to force wind into their sails.

His mind showed her a smaller vessel up ahead. Skipping through, she saw dangerous waves crashing into the smaller ship, and she heard screams as the people aboard were pitched from side to side.

There was no doubt in her mind—that was the bastard who took down the ship they'd found the remnants of.

"What the fuck are you doing?" the man who'd spoken to her before asked. "What are you doing with your eyes?"

She looked at him, the sclera of her eyes turning black, her pupils ringed in a smoky white. "Like I said, you should have used those legs to walk away when you had the chance. This is for all those you murdered and those you left for dead."

CHAPTER SIX

Once again, she opened her mind. Her suspicions were proven correct as she saw each of them had been aboard that ship and had been involved in sacking the smaller ship before killing men, women, and even children. They'd taken what they wanted and gone back to the safety of the Raider ship before their Caller finished off the other vessel, leaving those who were still alive to perish in the water and be ripped apart by the sharks and other marine predators.

She could feel the worry building in several people playing on the beach who had seen the men approach her. Worried they may get caught in the crossfire, Arryn sent out a mental warning. There were no words, only emotion.

Some grabbed their children and ran, others following suit when they saw people fearfully fleeing the beach. Within seconds, screaming erupted as the beach cleared.

Satisfied her message had been received and the rest would clear out before things got too bad, Arryn used the distraction to her advantage.

Her right hand shot out, twisting. The man in front of her screamed in pain as his knee gave, the horrible crunching sounds of the joint being crushed echoing around them as he hit the sand.

Arryn quickly turned to Corrine. "Can you use seaweed as well as you can vines?"

The little girl shook her head. "Not that good, but I can do whatever you have in mind."

The men charged, and Arryn nodded. "Good."

She flexed her body and a blast of telekinetic energy burst backward, throwing Corrine into the water. Arryn tumbled forward, snatching the sword from the man groaning on the ground and holding his broken knee. When she came back up, the men enclosed her, weapons drawn.

She allowed her magic to surround her, and with a loud *crack*, it transported her just outside the group. She rushed at them, feeling a chill in the air as the wind began to pick up. The Caller now stood ankle-deep in the water, the tip of his staff buried in the sand.

One of the three remaining men stepped forward and slashed at her with his sword. She arched back, dodging the blade that narrowly passed overhead, and raised her pilfered weapon to parry his next swing. The sound of the swords meeting rang in her ears. He was faster than she thought he'd be at his large size. He was able to land a hard punch on her face.

Everything spun, and her vision went blurry. Taking advantage of her disorientation, he punched her in the abdomen, eliciting a loud grunt. The pain radiated through her as she collapsed to the ground, her weapon falling beside her.

"Come here, you little bitch!"

Vision still blurry, she closed her eyes and opened her senses to feel for his movement. As he stepped forward, she jabbed her elbow into the soft tissue located at the front of his pants. He howled in both pain and anger as he stumbled back.

Arryn climbed shakily to her feet and planted her shoulder in his gut with a scream, knocking him to the ground, then began to punch him in the face. She connected twice but missed a third time when he grabbed a handful of her hair.

In a desperate attempt to level the playing field, she threw a handful of sand into his face to blind him. He cried out and bucked her off.

Senses on alert, she felt the other two as they ran for her. Though she couldn't see the sky, she could feel the darkness above and knew the Caller was ready to take action. She only wondered why he'd waited so long. More than enough time had passed for him to do serious damage.

Out on the water, Arryn could feel the swell of another's magic. Mariana had felt the power from the other Caller and now engaged.

Magic surrounded Arryn as a shield burst forth, her irises turning green as she began to heal herself. Her vision quickly returned, and when she thrust her hands directly in front of her, wind sent the two men flying backward. They tumbled over one another as they tried to keep their feet.

She spared a quick glance at the Caller and realized he'd been focused on Mariana's ship and the approaching boats, which were only a couple minutes at most from arriving.

"Corrine!" Arryn shouted as she stood and flung out her hand.

The man with the broken knee soared through the air and landed in the water. Corrine's eyes turned neon-green as seaweed rose from the depths and entangled the attacker. She started to pull him under, but Arryn stopped her.

"No! Leave them alive, just entangle them. Let Mariana and the others decide what to do."

Arryn felt a tingle in the air, and her hair began to stand on end. "Shit," she said out loud before jumping out of the way.

She moved just in time to avoid a bolt of lightning. Sand exploded everywhere and rained down on her. She turned, realizing the Caller had momentarily focused on her, but those aquamarine eyes had turned back toward the water. Arryn stood again.

At that moment, she realized she'd spent far more energy healing the victims from the water than she'd anticipated. It had been a long time since she'd received such a beating, and if those boats didn't arrive soon or if she didn't find a way to end it *fast*, she would be in serious trouble.

Everyone would be.

The blinded man on the ground had stumbled to his feet. Sword in hand, he began to swing it wildly. "I'll fucking kill you!"

Arryn shrugged, though he couldn't see it. Her eyes clouded over as she sent a quick thought to him, unable to help herself but smart enough not to give away her position.

You'll have to find me first, and I don't think that's going to happen anytime soon.

The other two men had climbed to their feet and ran forward with several feet between them. Arryn widened her stance, preparing to fight when she heard an angry battle cry.

Her eyes widened as she saw Corrine leap high enough in the air to do a flip and wrap her legs around the neck of one. She was small, but she sat upright before flinging her body back as hard as she could, yanking him off balance.

As he fell, she released him, landing on her hands and tumbling in a perfectly executed backflip as he hit the ground. Her eyes lit again as she thrust her hands forward, and a blast of energy radiated through Arryn that was hot enough to take her breath away as healing began.

Not wanting to waste the gift Corrine had given her, she took a confident step forward, her eyes flashing obsidian. Her hands arced over her chest and she pulled them away, a blue fireball glowing in each hand.

She hit the man running for her in the torso before throwing the other at the downed man, who had spun onto his stomach to go after Corrine. The fireball struck him hard in the back, and both men screamed as they rolled around on the ground.

A shaky Corrine stood, her neon-green eyes still glowing as she raised her hands and screamed again. Seaweed lifted above the surface and twisted around the ankles of each man, pulling them into the water and holding them there.

Arryn's eyes were wide as she watched the young girl, ferocious and strong, confidently fight alongside her.

Corrine looked over her shoulder to make sure her job had been done before glancing at Arryn and smiling. The girl blinked twice before her eyes rapidly faded to normal and she collapsed.

"Corrine!" Arryn called as she rushed to her side. "Damn it! *I'm* who's supposed to take care of *you*, not the other way around!"

Before she could focus on healing, she looked back to make sure the blinded man posed no threat. Then she felt the familiar tingle in the air. Looking around, she saw the sky had gone even darker. Focusing her energy, she once again allowed a barrier to form around her and Corrine just in time for lightning to come down all around them.

The sudden flash affected her vision, but she was able to blink away the worst of it after several seconds.

She saw the Caller once again turn toward the sea, and her still-blurred vision made out a dark smile on his face.

Her eyes widened when she realized why he'd waited so long to take action. He'd wanted a clear shot. So far, Arryn's group, Mariana, and the few men who traveled to shore with her had all been safe in the boats. A single lightning strike would not have been enough to kill them, and he'd wasted a lot of energy to keep Arryn pinned down. Now that they had all jumped into the water to run ashore, all of them could be killed with a single well-placed bolt.

As Arryn tried to stand within the barrier, ready to go after the Caller, lightning once again struck all around her and Corrine, preventing her from moving. She did her best to keep her eyes protected while covering Corrine's, but she couldn't take much more.

That bastard had them pinned, and she imagined that he'd assumed there wasn't much she could do.

Unfortunately for him, Arryn wasn't the type to give up easily.

Bast and Cleo used their incredible strength to leap from the water and soared toward the Raider. A flick of his wrist, the wind sent them flying far back, and they hit the water with a huge splash.

Arryn wasn't close enough to the water to control it, and doing it while keeping the barrier active would have been damn near impossible anyway.

As she tried to think of something, she felt Mariana's power swell, and lightning again webbed the sky. Arryn could feel the battle between them as they fought for control.

She saw Cathillian swim toward Bast and Cleo as the tigers rushed up the bank and ran to Arryn and Corrine. The men who'd accompanied Arryn's friends from the Storm Caller ship ran to help. Dante looked at the rogue Caller and Arryn sent him a silent warning through the bond, begging him not to go.

Thunder boomed overhead, and Arryn used all the energy she could spare to erect barriers around both large cats as they approached.

"Take her and get her out of here! She's fine, but she's unconscious. Get her somewhere safe, and I'll end this."

Snow nodded before lowering herself. Arryn lifted Corrine horizontally onto the tiger's back, the girl's arms hanging off one side and legs off the other. She was small enough that that was the best way for her to travel.

"Dante, run behind them and stabilize her if she starts to slip. *Go!*"

Each tiger growled in response, Dante giving her a quick, loving headbutt before rushing off behind his mother. Arryn watched them, doing her best to keep the barriers active as long as she could while lightning once again touched down all around.

She screamed as she shut her eyes to keep from being blinded. After the lightning faded and the thunder stopped booming, she saw that the tigers were out of sight. Her eyes wandered down to see blood on her hands. Reaching up, she touched her ears and pulled her fingers away to see more blood.

"This has to stop," she muttered.

Standing with her barrier still in place, she saw Mariana and the other Caller engaged in hand-to-hand combat. She hadn't realized Mariana had gotten so close.

Bast, Cleo, Cathillian, and Samuel were all on land, but they ran in the direction of the town. Echo's large shadow floated across the sand, and Arryn looked up to see her flying over a large group of men who had jumped into the fray.

Arryn's eyes flashed green as she healed herself again, her hearing quickly returning. She couldn't do a full heal, but it would be enough to get her going again.

Mariana, are you okay? Arryn sent to the Storm Caller.

I'm good. Go get the men coming to aid their Caller. The thunder alerted them to the fight.

The damage she'd suffered made her realize she hadn't been able to think or strategize. She hadn't even thought about the thunder alerting anyone from the Raider ship to come aid in battle. She'd been so focused that she hadn't thought of much of anything except surviving.

"If we make it out of this, I swear I'm going to take better care of myself," she said to herself. "No more stupid risks."

Her friends had told her more than a few times she'd gone far too hard for far too long, but she never listened. Now her actions had caught up to her.

That didn't mean she couldn't kick a few asses before unconsciousness took her as it had young Corrine.

She felt the energy swirling in the sky. The Callers battled for control, and it was painfully obvious that Arryn didn't have the power to come between them. Even at her strongest, she wasn't certain she could overtake either of their storms. While there were a few druids who could control the weather, Storm Callers grew up specifically training for that. That was *their* magic.

Metal clashed against metal, and Arryn dropped her barrier to rush into battle, hoping someone had brought her weapons. She groaned as she mentally kicked herself for leaving them on board. She hadn't wanted to get them in saltwater again and hadn't even considered the possibility they might run into the Raiders—or any other jerks—when they arrived.

A sandy tornado formed up ahead, and Arryn could see Bast and Cleo working in tandem to control it as it enveloped three men. They screamed as the sand scraped their skin and blinded them.

Running forward, Arryn leapt and planted her feet hard in the back of a man who'd just pulled a sword from its sheath as he prepared to go for Samuel. He lunged forward, stumbling, then Samuel swung his hammer and finished him off.

"Thanks, lassie. Ye look weak. Where's the wee one?"

Arryn righted herself and nodded. "I'm fine and so is Corrine, but we're definitely weak. I'm worried about Mariana. That bastard is *strong*."

Samuel nodded. "Then let's kill these bastards an' finish it."

Arryn opened her mouth to say something, but a pissed off and soaked snow rabbit darted past her, heading in the direction Snow and Dante had taken Corrine. She snuck a peek and was satisfied that he was okay, and so was Corrine. He just wanted to be near her since he was her familiar.

A scream tore through the air, and Arryn looked over to see Mariana fall into the water. The other Caller pulled a sword from her torso, and Arryn knew if the woman wasn't dead already, she didn't have long.

"Arryn, go!" Bast yelled as she pulled Arryn's bow from her

back and threw it in her direction. Arryn hadn't even noticed the Kemetian carrying it.

"Here," Cleo said as she ran up, handing her the quiver. "They got wet when we were thrown into the water, but they're here, and so are most of the arrows. I owe you a few."

"Thank you," Arryn said before picking her bow up off the ground and grabbing the quiver from Cleo.

"He'll see you coming a mile away," Cleo said. "You're gonna have to confuse him. From what Mariana said, they're not used to physical magic. Overwhelm him with it. Your nature magic is useless here with all the sand, and anything weather-related… Well, he can kick your ass at it. No offense."

Arryn nodded, her eyes flashing black as she turned back toward the Caller, who now focused on all of them. "Why the hell aren't you exhausted by now?" she asked no one in particular. If that had been her, she'd have passed out after using all that magic.

Taking deep breaths to steel herself, Arryn allowed her magic to surround her again. "If this works, I will owe Corrine for giving me the energy boost."

Before Cleo could respond, Arryn allowed her magic to implode around her, transporting her behind the Caller. She pulled an arrow from the quiver, nocked it, and let it fly. Her opponent turned in the water, a blast of wind sending the arrow off-course and into the sea.

A familiar tingle in the air sent shivers down her spine, and she quickly teleported out of the water to another location before he could call a lightning strike that would more than likely kill Mariana. Cleo had said to overwhelm him with her physical magic, but she wasn't sure she had enough energy to continue teleporting all over to try and fail to shoot him. Getting close enough to strike him by hand seemed impossible as well.

When he turned toward the group again, his storm clouds growing as lightning webbed across the sky, she knew he planned to take all of them out—even his own men if he had to.

Looking over, Arryn saw Mariana slowly pulling herself to shore, watching his every move. The woman's life force was fading fast.

Chills raced through the druid and her panic grew as Cleo's words rang through Arryn's mind. *Your nature magic is useless here.* She realized physical magic wasn't much better. He could counter anything she did with wind.

But she bet he'd never met a mystic before.

A distant coldness wrapped around Arryn as her emotions took hold, her eyes turning white. Vague memories of things Margit had taught her, things she'd seen Zoe do, and stories she'd been told about Julianne raced through her mind. She imagined herself standing several feet in front of the Caller, and as the first bolt of lightning was called, she saw an image of herself appear in a cloud of smoke directly in front of her opponent.

She'd startled him enough that he missed his mark, sand and dirt exploding where the bolt had struck the ground.

In another breath, another illusion of her appeared, an arrow nocked as the image pulled back. The Caller thrust a hand to the sky, and lightning crashed around him as he tried to strike at something that didn't exist.

The images faded as more appeared. Arryn was pulled from her trance when she heard a weak Mariana scream her name.

Arryn looked over to see the woman's eyes pleading with her to stop. She knew how much magic Arryn had used to heal the injured back on the ship, and she understood that this was dangerous.

Blinking a few times, Arryn shook her head and pulled another arrow from the quiver as her illusions rushed at the Caller. He fought wildly, thrusting with his sword and missing. She could feel his panic rising as she pulled back a real arrow.

This is for all the innocents you took from this world, she sent to him as she loosed the arrow.

It whistled through the air and struck the confused and overwhelmed Caller in the back of the neck. He fell to his knees before falling face-first into the water. The skies almost immediately cleared, and Arryn rushed as quickly as she could manage to Mariana.

She fell to her knees in the water, almost tipping the rest of the way over from weakness. As she placed her shaky hands on Mariana's abdomen, Mariana gently grabbed them.

"No. I'm not sure you won't kill yourself if you use any more magic."

Arryn shook her head lightly, her will to stay awake quickly fading. "I have to. I'm not going to let you die."

Arryn's eyes flashed green as she pushed healing magic through to Mariana, but within a few heartbeats, her eyes fluttered closed as darkness took her.

CHAPTER SEVEN

Arryn's eyes slowly opened. She closed them, wishing she was unconscious again. Her entire body ached, and her head felt as though it might split apart at any moment.

"Ugh. I think I might have overdone it," she moaned, trying to roll to her side. She felt the wet sand under her fingers and the memory of trying to heal Mariana before she'd passed out slammed into her. Her eyes shot open, and she searched frantically. "Mariana—is she alive? Did I get to her in time?"

"*Shhh.*" Cathillian leaned forward and ran a gentle hand down her cheek. "She's fine. You bought her enough time for me to get to her. Still in some pain since I had to heal you both, but she'll be just fine."

Arryn sighed heavily in relief and fell back to the sand again. "I'm so glad. How's Corrine? Have Snow and Dante returned with her?"

"She's fine, too. Stop worrying. You need to worry about yourself. You definitely overdid it. The fight with Esmerelda... It might have been a couple weeks ago, but as hard as you've been going over the last year, your body is worn down. You never give yourself time to recover.

"A good night's sleep is plenty for me to recharge, but you? Not even close, but you act like it is. One or two nights, and you're back at it. I don't think you ever fully recovered from the fight, then you spent a lot of energy healing the people we found in the water, and now this." He gave his own heavy sigh. "You can't keep doing this to yourself. There *will* come a time when you're not so lucky, you know?"

She nodded, keeping her sensitive eyes closed to protect them from the sun. "I know. Trust me, after that one, I know. I was fully confident I was going to kick the asses of four guys. I've taken on *far* worse odds and come out on top. I looked at them like I was facing down a few scrawny teenagers. I got *way* too cocky. They were a lot faster and stronger than I expected, and it cost me dearly."

"You've always been overly confident. It's one of the things I love about you. But—" he took a deep breath, "I don't want it to cost you your life, you know? You probably would have been fine if you'd been taking better care of yourself, but you haven't been. I haven't said anything because I didn't want to overstep, but I am now, and I'll continue to do so."

She gently grabbed the hand stroking her wet hair. "Thank you. Don't ever be afraid to tell me when I've gone too far. We both know I'd be the first one to tell you that you're acting like a total jackass."

Cathillian laughed. "Of course, you'd be the one to ruin a serious moment."

She shrugged. "You knew that before you annoyed me into a relationship."

"Aye, she'll be just fine."

Arryn smiled and peeked through squinted eyes to see Samuel come to a stop several feet away. "Did ya get 'em all, Sam? Bitch knows this one needed the help."

"Hey!" Cathillian lightly slapped her shoulder. "You're mean."

"Just to you." She tried to wink at him, but it was unsuccessful, given her squinted eyes. She forced herself over onto her stomach and slowly got to her knees. Looking around, she only saw half her group. "Where is everyone?"

"You've been out for about two hours. I healed you while Echo led the twins to Corrine and the other familiars. Samuel helped Mariana and what was left of her crew get the living Raiders bound and thrown in the boats. She wanted to stick around, but they needed to locate the Raider ship to take it back home."

"Hmm. I was wondering why I didn't see another ship," Arryn said, looking around the now calm beach.

"There are many coves around here for them to hide a ship in. They do that when coming to port, so if their ship is found, they aren't, and vice versa."

She nodded. "I see." Her eyes darted to his. "Wait a minute. I was out for two *hours*? You left me lying here, half in the water, for two *hours*?"

He laughed. "Yes, I did! And before you continue to get angry about it, I had a good reason." He paused and she quirked an eyebrow at him, silently urging him to continue. He chuckled again. "After healing the survivors in the water, none of us had much left. I didn't have much to give you anyway, not after healing Mariana. I healed you and realized you were healing faster than usual while lying in the water. I thought it might be because of those lessons I taught you a while back, so I left you here and helped the others. You were never in danger or uncomfortable."

"Mmhmm. Next time you're injured, I'll chuck you in a tree. When anyone asks, I'll just say, 'Oh, it's fine. He loves it there. He's close to nature. He'll heal just fine.'"

His head fell back as he let loose with a loud bark of laughter.

"I don't think ye'll win this one, lad," Samuel said.

Arryn pointed at the rearick. "That's a smart man. All right, well, everyone is safe and sound. Mariana is alive and back on her ship, where she's strongest. I was told this place has food. Let's go find it because I'm starving. I need food and sleep."

Cathillian and Samuel helped her to her feet. She felt wobbly and drunk, but she was able to walk on her own. Their horses stood on the bank, their coats glistening in the sun. Maia had sand all over her damp coat, and Arryn imagined it was from rolling around on the ground and in the water.

Wet and sandy herself, Arryn allowed Cathillian to help her onto Maia's back before riding toward town. It didn't take long to get there, and Arryn was happy to see the rest of her crew.

Bast, Cleo, and Corrine sat just outside the town with Snow, Dante, and the rabbit huddled around them. She smiled when she saw them. Corrine's dark skin looked a little pale, but otherwise, she seemed perfectly fine.

Arryn carefully slid off Maia's back and walked over to Corrine, who stood on shaky legs to give her a hug. "I'm glad you're okay," the druid said. "If it weren't for you, I wouldn't have managed like I did."

Corrine squeezed her tight enough that her body shook, and Arryn could feel how weak she was. "You needed me. I knew I could help."

Smiling, Arryn looked down at her. "Well, you've certainly gotten stronger. You pushed an incredible amount of healing power through me. It was hot enough to take my breath away."

"I told you I'm strong enough to fight with you. I took that guy down all by myself."

"Yeah, we'll discuss that part later. For now, we need food and rest," Arryn said, placing her hands on Corrine's shoulders and turning her toward town.

"So, you came through here before?" Cathillian asked the twins. "What place had good food?"

Cleo shrugged. "There are a couple places. We ate at one, and they had good food. It's a little... adult, but the barkeep keeps people in line." She pointed down the street. "The tamer one's down that way, but it looks kind of busy."

Arryn hadn't seen so many people wandering around since her time in Arcadia. The city in the Valley was much larger, but there were hundreds of people walking about.

She saw merchants of every kind lined up on the streets, selling fruit, vegetables, bolts of cloth, bags and containers, weapons, clothing, and more. The inn Bast and Cleo pointed out had people pouring in as several exited. They'd never get service before the exhaustion took her and Corrine.

"Is anythin' down there?" Samuel asked. "Seems ta be pretty calm."

"Yeah. That's where the other one is. It wouldn't hurt to walk around and see if we can find something else," Bast said.

Arryn and Corrine groaned. "Speak for yourself," Arryn said.

Corrine's head flopped back. "I'm a druid. Nudity does *not* bother me, especially female nudity. In case ya haven't noticed, I'm a girl. I know what it all looks like. Feed me before I punch something."

Arryn snorted, and Cathillian outright laughed. He nudged Arryn's shoulder. "That's *definitely* your kid. I could almost swear you birthed her yourself."

Snow rubbed her face on Arryn's arm and she turned. The big cat's crystalline blue eyes stared into hers as she pushed sympathy through the bond. She knew Arryn needed the help and wanted her to accept it. The tiger lowered herself to the ground, and Arryn climbed on as gasps filled the air.

"Relax," Cleo said in a loud, annoyed tone. "No one get your pants in a bunch. They're tame. Just don't fuck with the girls on their backs, and you'll keep your heads."

Arryn chuckled, hearing the dark sense of humor and sarcasm in Cleo's voice. She looked over to see Cathillian help Corrine onto Dante's back.

"Okay," Arryn said. "Now we can go down the less busy streets."

Echo called as she circled around, ever the guardian in the skies. "She says everything seems calm," Cathillian reported.

They made their way through the crowd, which wasn't difficult with two white tigers that were as large as a lot of the horses around. People parted and talked about the beautiful beasts as they passed. A few children burst away from their parents and through the loiterers to risk a pet.

Arryn smiled when Snow and Dante lovingly chuffed at the kids before they were snatched up by their mothers. Soon, the crowd thinned, and they were able to travel freely to the opposite end of the long street, where they found a few stores and another inn and restaurant.

"Here we go!" Arryn said, her stomach growling as she smelled the food from outside. She looked back at the twins. "I smell beef. I'm sure this is the place you described as being rough around the edges, but I'm risking it."

She slid off Snow and made her way inside with her friends. As they crossed the threshold, Arryn quickly realized the establishment was exactly as described. It was less than family-oriented. Barely dressed women served drinks, and a drunk man stumbled down the steps as he buttoned his pants, a scantily clad woman not far behind him.

"Well, this is just wonderful," Arryn said.

"*Mmhmm*. Yes, it is," Cathillian said, his eyes wandering around the room.

Arryn smiled and shook her head. "If you want to keep those eyes, I'd suggest keeping them on something safe."

"Please," Corrine said with a yawn. "There's not a single nipple anywhere. Let's just get some food and go to sleep."

Arryn wanted to laugh because she'd never heard Corrine be so blunt and forceful before. She knew the girl was exhausted, and that was fueling her lack of filter.

"I'm with her," Bast said. "Besides, like we said before, the barkeep keeps it tame downstairs. It's the shit that happens *up*stairs we want to avoid."

"Ye don't speak fer everybody, lass," Samuel mumbled, and Cathillian chuckled.

Arryn nodded and walked up to the bar. "Hello. My friends and I need a few rooms that haven't been...*occupied* recently. And food. Lots of food."

The bartender stacked a glass he'd just dried, and looked up, giving Arryn a gentle smile. She had never seen skin as dark as his. The darkness softened his features and made him look like he'd never seen a blemish in his life, though she doubted that to be true, especially in his profession. She imagined a lot of assholes came through, and he was stunning.

"No worries, ma'am. This place is bigger than it looks. Regular rooms are downstairs. We can get you set up and comfortable, and I can have someone bring your food to you." He pointed behind her, and she turned to see a passed-out Corrine in Cathillian's arms. The large cats laid on either side of the door just inside. "She doesn't look like she'd make it through a meal anyway."

Arryn nodded. "Neither one of us will, but we need to try." Turning back to face him, she caught him staring at someone. "Everything okay?"

"Mm. Yes," he said, obviously concentrating on something. He nodded his head in the direction he stared in. "Be careful of that one over there in all black sitting with his friend. He's been eyeballing you since you walked in."

An audible sigh escaped her. "No offense, but in a place like this, I'm not surprised."

His eyes met hers. "None taken. This is my place. I realize it doesn't look like much, but I make sure it stays safe. The women who work here do so by choice. The rules are, *they* pick. The patrons can look, but they don't touch unless they're invited to buy. I don't take kindly to people taking or touching things or people without permission."

"That's very good to know. I have a very strong code I follow as well, so we should get along just fine."

As she looked into his eyes, she realized she couldn't sense anything bad about him. He seemed very genuine and almost calming. Though she'd judged the place harshly when she walked in, she felt confident they would be safe enough while there.

He turned and waved someone over before meeting her gaze again. "I'm Amon," he said, pausing as a woman in her early twenties with beautiful dark hair with kinky curls walked up. "This is Hasina. She will take you to your rooms and bring your food to you."

The woman smiled brightly. She had green eyes the color of Cathillian's but medium-dark skin like Corrine's. Like her boss, she radiated positive energy.

"I'll get you taken care of." She looked at Amon. "What about the tigers?"

He laughed. "In my travels, I've seen tigers. I've seen the largest breeds the continent had to offer, but I've never seen *anything* like them."

Arryn smiled. "They're my familiars. I'd prefer they stay with me, but if that can't happen, anywhere shaded and close will work. They won't hurt anything."

"You're sure about that?" Amon asked.

She nodded. "They aren't like normal tigers, and they aren't trained." She tapped her temple. "Druids have a connection to their familiars. They understand what we say. If they're hungry, they'll tell me. They share the same code you and I have. They don't like people touching things or others that don't belong to them. As long as no one poses a threat to anyone else, especially kids, they won't hurt a soul."

"Well, I don't want to say the stables, but that's about the only place we have available that would suit them. There's fresh water out there, and I can take them some scrap meat we have in the back," he said.

"That will be just fine as long as they aren't penned in. No gates."

"I'll see to that myself," he said.

She nodded. "Thank you. They can stay with our horses. I appreciate your hospitality. What do we owe you?"

He paused, clearly thinking over his words as he stared into her eyes. "I was wondering if I might ask a favor instead of payment. It's a big one."

"I'm listening," she said.

"I have a feeling you might be druids, at least a few of you. Your blonde friend has the ears, though yours have a slight point as well, I see. When you confirmed it, I knew I had to take a chance. One of the girls working here...Maria. Her eleven-year-old son has been sick. We don't have a diagnosis, but he's getting worse. The doctors say he won't see his fifteenth birthday if things don't change. If you'd be willing to help him, you can have the room and the food for free. Just tip Hasina whenever she comes to help you. I don't want to take from her, but anything house-related, it's on me."

"I might have enough left in me," Cathillian said, standing just behind Arryn.

Amon shook his head. "I won't risk your health. He'll be fine for tonight. I don't know what happened earlier, but I could sense it. You've used too much magic already. Get some sleep. We'll take care of you tonight, and tomorrow when you wake, I'll take you to him."

"Thank you," Arryn said.

Amon bowed his head slightly. "It's no trouble. Thank *you*—more than you know. Again, I know we don't look like much here, but we take care of each other. You have to with all the dangers in the world these days."

She offered a gentle smile, though her body was about to give out on her. She needed food and sleep soon, or she would collapse. Still, she needed to make sure he understood her limits.

"I will do anything I can to help that boy, but you should know there are limits going into this." When she paused, he looked at her with full attention. "We can heal wounds, headaches, and acute illnesses that pop up. Anything that is chronic or lifelong, we can heal the damage but not the cause. It *will* come back, but it will take a while."

His shoulders slumped. "So, it would be a bandage. He would get sick again."

She nodded. "Yes. That being said, it will take years for that to happen. A vacation to the Dark Forest every five or so years wouldn't be the *worst* thing, would it?"

His face brightened, and a smile spread across his face. "Yes. I think you're right." His deep brown eyes glistened. "Thank you for the honesty. You're free to stay as long as you need to. If it's longer than a day or two, though, we will need to work together on a plan to feed the tigers."

She nodded. "No problem there. Should be two days at most, though if you know of any farms around with cattle, we could use one. I doubt we'll find many large wild animals in the desert."

"I'll see what I can do," he said. He turned to the young woman beside him. "Hasina, please make sure they're comfortable."

She nodded enthusiastically. "I will. Follow me, please!"

After stepping out from behind the bar, she took them on a weaving path through the bar, trying to avoid the patrons. As they walked, Arryn spotted the man Amon had warned her about. Given how everyone was positioned, she had no choice but to follow Hasina around that table.

There was a curvy light-skinned woman with dark-blonde hair and blue eyes placing drinks on his table, so she hoped he would be distracted.

As soon as she passed him, she felt a hard smack on the right side of her ass, and the loud *thwap!* resonated in the air.

She spun but wasn't fast enough. The blonde serving the table grabbed him by the hair and slammed him face-first into the table. She'd let go as soon as he made contact, so his head bounced back far enough for Arryn to see the blood spurt from his nose.

A laugh threatened to burst from her at any moment, so she bit her lip.

"Big fucking no-no," the blonde said. "You don't touch *anyone* here unless you're invited to, and she doesn't even work here."

Arryn felt his rage spike as the man shoved his chair back and rose. The blonde woman stood strong, not an ounce of fear on her face as the man who was nearly a foot taller than her at his full height took a step toward her.

As tired as she was, Arryn's reflexes kicked in, and she took a step forward. That woman had defended her, and she wasn't about to let her take any abuse for her sake.

However, the druid didn't have time to retaliate before the man began to scream and clutch the sides of his head. He fell to his knees, his screams turning into loud groans.

"You know the rules in my bar," Amon said, his deep voice booming across the room.

Everyone quieted, and Arryn looked over to see the bartender's normally deep brown eyes a steel-bluish gray. She could sense the mental magic he used, but it was different. She understood then why he'd been so knowledgeable about her magic-induced fatigue.

"Leave now and never return," Amon said. "You won't lay rough hands on women in my bar, and if I ever catch sight of you doing it anywhere else? Well, I promise I won't be as *friendly* about it as I am being right now."

The screams stopped, and the man on the floor stood almost robotically. Amon had full control over his mind, and she watched with interest as the lecherous man made his way through the bar and out the door.

Turning back to Amon, she saw his eyes fade back to normal and a smile spread across his face. "No one will harm any of you here. I protect everyone within my establishment. Please rest easy."

Arryn liked him, and she was happy to see her intuition about him hadn't been wrong.

"Sorry about that," Hasina said, drawing Arryn's attention back her way. "Let's get you guys to your room, where you can get some sleep."

Arryn sighed heavily. "I've never heard anything so great in all my life."

CHAPTER EIGHT

The days were long and exhausting, working in the tunnels, but everything had gone according to plan so far. Asim and the others had just finished their shift and walked out into the hot Kemetian weather. She couldn't wait to take a cool bath to soothe her sore body.

The men and women who came out of the tunnel wiped sweat off their brows. She knew they were famished. Her stomach had roared every few minutes in the last hour of work, and she couldn't wait to get something to eat.

The Kemetian sands were far too deep to dig down to the bedrock below, but the ground under the city was fairly solid, thanks to being close to the great river. Digging north hadn't caused any issues so far, and as long as they stayed on their path, their tunnels would remain stable.

While Asim hoped the girls would return home soon, she was confident her plan would work if the worst were to happen.

As she headed toward tables set with enough food to feed an army, she was halted by a frantic voice calling from behind her, "My queen!"

She turned to see a guard named Jabril rushing toward her. "Yes, what is it?"

The soldier took several heaving breaths before pointing toward the western gates. "Bodies." He panted twice more before clearing his throat. "Several of our soldiers were found slain."

Asim stepped forward and allowed him to take a few more breaths. He'd come quite a distance in the hot desert air, so she wanted him to have a moment to calm down.

"Are you all right?" she asked.

Jabril straightened and nodded. "Yes, Your Highness. Forgive me."

She waved a hand, trying to stay calm but losing her patience. "What happened? Was it the demons to the south?"

The soldier shook his head. "No. We discovered them on patrol. At first, we worried it might be them—the monsters—but we ruled that out the moment we saw the wounds. Those were human kills."

Her jaw clenched as she stared into Jabril's eyes. In the last several months, she had seen more than her fair share of death, and she'd heard about much more. Kemet was not the same place it had once been.

It had begun to evolve from a misogynistic society to accepting women among the working and even in the ranks. With a queen instead of a king, many changes had taken effect, changes she'd been scared to implement but had pushed because of the strength in her daughters.

Together, they had changed the kingdom. Asim believed in their direction, but it had been short-lived. Only a few short years had passed before *they* came—the beasts to the south. They'd torn holes into this world from somewhere else.

Asim knew magic existed and used it herself, but she'd never seen magic strong enough to rip gaping holes through this world to connect to another. Many travelers, missionaries, and master magicians of different schools of magic had come through her gates, but no one had *ever* mentioned anything like that.

Ancient religions and beliefs passed down from generation to generation still existed to some extent. She'd heard of "planes of existence." She wondered if maybe hell itself had opened.

Her mind reeled as she thought about how so many terrifying things could have taken place around them, and people still found reasons to kill one another.

"So much death around us, hanging over us, and they choose to do the job for the invaders." Her fists clenched. "Show me."

Asim grabbed a roll from the table to calm her aching stomach as the soldier led her across the city to the gates. Just inside were four bodies with different wounds.

"Did they think we wouldn't discover them? Did they think we wouldn't retaliate?" the queen asked.

"We don't know," Jabril responded. "I do know their weapons are gone, as well as anything valuable."

Asim shook her head. "Everyone in my kingdom has been invited to live within the city walls. I offered safety. They would have food, water, and other resources. They don't have to fight to survive. Why? Why would they do this?"

A soldier with dark skin and green eyes stepped forward and bowed. "My queen."

"Yes, Shai?" she said. "Do you have more information?"

Shai stood and nodded. "I believe so. I've questioned several outsiders, and they remain loyal to you and to the kingdom. I believe them. Unfortunately, I think there is more to the story." He sighed before continuing. "The first home I visited wasn't shy about telling me of a man they believe has ill intentions toward the kingdom. They said he was kind and friendly, but he gave them a bad feeling. When I asked the other houses, some denied knowing anything, but I could tell they were lying—about that anyway."

"Lying? Why would they lie? And why would you trust them if

you'd caught them in lies?" she asked. Shai had always been a good judge of character, which was why she always placed him on patrol or as her personal guard. She trusted him, but that didn't mean she wouldn't question him.

"They didn't seem afraid. They almost seemed protective, but their demeanor changed between talking about the strange man, who they called Zuri, and talking about the murders. Their posture was stiff while discussing the man. Everything else, they were far more relaxed. Whoever that man is, he has their trust. They know who he is but won't say anything. I had no reason to doubt anything else they said, but they lied about knowing anything about the stranger."

"What did the others say about him?" Asim asked.

"That's the interesting part. The last house I visited said they didn't know who he was, but he'd visited them. Offered them protection in exchange for their help. It seems he's raising an army of his own. They made sure to say he was very nice and seemed genuinely concerned about them and the area as a whole. He gave them no indication he was lying, but something didn't sit right with them. They said he seemed *too* nice, which they found suspicious. They even mentioned they didn't want to alarm anyone or get anyone in trouble over what they said because they had nothing more than a gut feeling to go on.

"They didn't know why he wanted the help, and they didn't want to know. They'd left the city because they believed the demons would go after larger areas with more people. Their theory is more noise, more smells, bigger target. They said if they wanted to be sitting ducks in a large group again, they'd come back to the city."

Asim thought for several moments. "From the limited information you gathered, do you think this man is putting together an army as a way to protect the outsiders from the monsters? Or do you believe he's a threat to the kingdom as a whole?"

The queen already knew the answer to that. The bodies in

front of her told her everything she needed to know. Still, she prided herself on getting the opinions of others so she could see a larger picture than the one she'd painted in her own mind.

Shai shook his head. "It's impossible to know for sure without finding him and speaking to him myself, but I would say he's a threat. I find all this too coincidental. We find dead soldiers at the same time we learn of a stranger in the area recruiting people. An attack on a soldier is an attack on Jadid. It doesn't matter if an outsider originally came from within our walls, that's common sense. In my humble opinion, this needs further investigation."

Jabril stepped up to her right. "I agree. I don't think a stranger showing up and asking people to help him defend the land against the monsters is cause to worry. After all, our men have all been pulled away to help with the construction of the tunnels and for security, due to increased traffic coming in from the south. It's not farfetched to think the people would band together to protect themselves.

"That being said, two of the places you visited feeling compelled to lie about it is what concerns me. That man had other plans. I'm almost certain of it. Regardless, a hunch isn't enough to convict. We need to look into this further."

Asim nodded. "That was my thought, but I wanted to get your opinion. We need to come up with a plan. I want to lure this man out. Find him and find out what he's doing. Organically. We don't want to scare him off, and if he does mean well, we don't want to threaten him. I think subtlety is what's needed here."

Both soldiers bowed. "Yes, Your Highness."

"First thing, we need to get these bodies taken care of and the families notified. They will have a proper burial and be shown all the respect they and their families are owed. After the bodies are prepared and the families are notified, please get some food. We'll figure out what to do about this…stranger."

She gave a curt nod before turning to the bodies, then closed her eyes and respectfully bowed. "Thank you for your service and your bravery," she said at normal volume. As she straightened, she lowered her voice. "We will get the bastards who did this to you, mark my words. Rest in peace, knowing that."

Asim made her way back toward the palace so she could eat and plan. Losing in battle was one thing, but this was quite another. It was obvious they had been snuck up on and taken without much fight, and she wasn't about to let that stranger and his group of assholes get away with cold-blooded murder.

CHAPTER NINE

Though the half-moon was high overhead, some of the earlier heat still clung to the air. Soon, it would disappear altogether and be replaced by a chill. After a hearty meal and nearly an hour spent planning, Asim went to get some sleep while Jabril and Shai set out to ready their men.

After the sun went down completely, Asim rose and readied herself for another long night. This time, she wouldn't be sleeping but instead out with her soldiers.

Jabril and Shai had educated guesses as to where the stranger might go next, based on the path he'd taken through the houses and small villages he'd visited. While there wasn't a clear pattern, they were able to narrow it down to three places he might go.

Asim ordered Jabril and Shai to take teams of soldiers and go to the first and second potential targets. They were to request entrance, and only Jabril and Shai would go inside, while their teams hid in the shadows outside.

If the stranger showed at either location, Jabril or Shai would play the part of the man of the house and have a conversation with him to learn whatever they could before they and their men engaged. The goal was to get as much information as possible but not let the stranger or anyone with him leave.

Asim went to the final house, but she remained outside, allowing her closest Queen's Guard Faraj to go inside. While no one knew anything about the stranger, Asim assumed he was older and part of the group that had been resistant to the changes she'd made. He only spoke to men, which told her enough to make what she thought was a reasonable assumption.

After climbing onto the roof where she would be safe, she looked around to make sure everyone was in position. Had she not known where her guards were, she wouldn't have seen them. Her men agreed this was the location least likely to be visited, and they'd demanded their queen go there.

While she didn't care about danger and was confident in her abilities as well as those of her guardsmen, she acquiesced, knowing it was her duty to her people to stay alive.

If she died, Bast and Cleo would rise to power the moment they returned to Kemet. Neither was ready, and neither wanted it yet. They weren't finished growing up and finding who they were as individuals. She would do anything to make sure they got that chance before it was their time.

"My Queen!" someone whispered loudly from below.

She reached out with her power, but she was too far away from the earth to sense any changes. "What is it?" she called back in the same fashion.

"We have incoming."

"Alert Faraj. Quickly!" she ordered.

Within seconds, she heard someone scratching on the window at the back of the house. It was far less obvious than knocking, and it worked beautifully. She heard the soft creak of the window as it opened and quiet whispers from below. While she couldn't sense the vibrations in the ground that her guard had sensed, she could feel Faraj making his way through the small farmhouse.

Asim looked around but saw nothing and no one. This particular home sat on a patch of land that was close enough to the Nile that rich, black earth supported its livestock and crops. A good portion of the crops brought into the city were purchased from farmers like the one here and others along the river.

That was why her soldiers had assumed this location would be the least likely to be hit. No farmer would willingly leave his land or risk it, so why would the stranger try to recruit one? So far, it seemed recruitment was his goal. Theft and devastation hadn't yet been a problem.

She wondered if that was about to change.

Within two minutes, Asim saw horses coming across the land. There were more than ten, but from that distance, she couldn't get an accurate headcount. She flattened herself on the peak of the roof and slid down the back enough that she would not be seen. It felt as though time stood still while she waited for something to happen.

After what felt like an eternity, she heard the noisy horses come to a stop and several men talking. She badly wanted to pull herself up to look over the peak and see how many men there were, but she remained still. She wouldn't have to hide like a coward for long.

There were several sharp knocks on the front door, and Faraj's footsteps vibrated through the home as he moved to the door.

"Good evening," Faraj said. "It's quite late. What can I do for you men?"

"I assume you own this home," a man with a deep voice said.

He didn't sound angry or threatening, but she couldn't see them, so she decided to wait to pass judgment.

"That I do. Have you come for food? We have plenty if you're hungry," Faraj responded in a friendly tone.

"That's not why we're here. Well, not *entirely*. We do need supplies, but we also want to ask you a few questions."

There was a pause. "A few questions?" Faraj asked. She was impressed by how well he acted.

"Yeah. I'm sure you're aware the desert has become...*hostile.*"

Her hands cramped from holding on so she didn't slide, but it wasn't anything she couldn't handle. The gradient was light enough that she didn't have to hold much of her weight, but it was still painful.

Hurry the hell up, she thought.

"Given those beasts out there, that's a friendly way of putting it, I'd say," Faraj replied.

"Exactly. It's been scary, and it's only gonna get worse. We've discovered some very unsettling news. It affects all of us, but it affects people like you directly. We're hoping you'll help us solve this problem before it becomes too much."

"Oh, no." There was a pause and some rustling. She heard the front door creak shut, and she felt Faraj's footsteps move onto the covered front porch. "Sorry about that. I don't want my wife and daughter to hear. What's going on?"

"We found several soldiers patrolling a little too far from Jadid. Turns out, they weren't patrolling at all," the man with the deep voice said.

"They were inspecting the area," a man with a higher voice said. He didn't sound much older than seventeen, but she couldn't be sure without looking.

"Inspecting the area? For what?" Faraj asked.

"They're scouting to figure out where they can get the most supplies in an emergency. The queen is panicking and preparing for the apocalypse. I'm telling you, she's coming for all of us."

"What!" Faraj exclaimed, shock in his voice. She was pretty sure it was genuine. "Why would she do that? We give the city anything they need."

"Because we're all out here alone. They're in that damned city with their tall walls and an army to protect them. What happens if the queen gets paranoid about these monsters? She'll order land to be seized! She'll take whatever resources she needs to feed her family and her legion of worshippers. Those soldiers have proven that."

"How does a handful of patrolling soldiers prove that?" Faraj asked.

She could hear the disbelief in his voice, and she prayed he'd hold it back for a little bit longer. She wanted to go down there and punch that guy in the face, but she couldn't without giving everything away.

"Because they attacked us. We patrol too. Our priority has been to protect our lands since the queen pulled back all the soldiers. We make sure the monsters don't attack, and we make sure the people around here aren't hurting anyone. Recently, because of what we've seen, that careful watch has extended to the queen's men.

"We saw strange men on our land, and we went to find out why. It has never been illegal or even ill-advised to approach a soldier. When we got close enough to see that was what they were, we started to back off, but they had other plans. They attacked us for no reason. Fortunately, we were able to come out ahead. I'm not proud of it, but we got one to talk, and he told me the queen has them scouting the land."

"Straight from the horse's mouth," the higher-voiced man said, backing his friend up.

"Exactly. How can we argue when they told us that themselves?"

Lying bastards, she thought. Those soldiers had no defensive wounds. She'd suspected as much, but the medical examiner had confirmed it after the bodies had been cleaned. Her soldiers had been executed. They were snuck up on and taken. She had no idea how that had happened, but it had.

The men below had failed to recruit people the old-fashioned way and were now resorting to fear tactics. They were trying to turn her people against her and the kingdom. She suspected that wouldn't work on those closer to the city, but it would only need to work on a few to start an unnecessary war in the midst of an already terrifying time.

She heard chattering among the other men who'd arrived with the two talking to Faraj. Fear settled in her belly as she heard rocks shifting on the left side of the house.

"Excuse me," he shouted around. "Gotta piss." The man took a few more steps around the side. "What the fuck? Who the hell are you!"

"Shit," she said out loud as a fight ensued.

Her men leapt from the shadows below, and she pulled herself all the way up to the peak to prepare for battle. While she had no way of knowing if any of the men below was the dangerous stranger they'd been warned about, she knew for sure they were assholes preying on the weak, or at the very least, the gullible.

You'll regret this, she thought as she slid down the front of the roof and down onto the porch cover. *You'll all regret this.*

CHAPTER TEN

The moment Faraj heard the man around the side of the house call out, he reached for the sheathed knife he had attached to the back of his pants. He moved like lightning as he thrust it into the side of the lying bastard standing in front of him. Out of the corner of his eye, he saw several men rush around the side of the house, but he couldn't do anything about it. His focus needed to be right where it was.

Rage washed through him as he thought of what those men had tried to do. They'd assumed he was a farmer and probably not very smart, and they'd wanted to use him. They wanted to turn him into a weapon and take his supplies.

What if they hadn't been there? What if the real farmer had not agreed to join? They'd come for the supplies, and Faraj had no doubt in his mind they would have left with whatever they'd come for. He became angrier when he thought of what those men would have done to get them.

Every word that had come from his opponent's mouth had been carefully planned before they'd arrived. So many lies, all so they could recruit an army dedicated to a false cause.

He hadn't had much time to figure out why because of the random man who had walked around the edge of the house to piss. Silent hopes had filled Faraj's mind that he wouldn't discover the soldiers, but they were quickly dashed.

He needed to end this before the queen was injured. His goal was to maim without killing if possible. They needed answers before anything like this happened again.

Pulling the knife free, he stepped back and swiftly kicked the man's knee, forcing him to the ground. His opponent fell, a choked, pain-filled groan escaping his throat as he struggled to grab his side with one hand and his knee with the other.

As he turned to the other three men standing on the porch with him, his senses picked up vibrations moving through the house as the family inside ran to the back room and the queen slid down the front of the roof to stand on the porch roof above him.

Faraj ducked and sheathed his blade as the first man threw a punch. Thrusting his arms out, Faraj was able to shove him off-balance as he worked to defend himself against the next man. Not killing them made the fight more difficult, but he would stick to the plan if he could.

His new opponent was taller and broader, built much like the unfortunate fellow on the ground he'd had such an enlightening conversation with before things went south.

As Faraj had expected, his opponent used his size to his advantage instead of talent. He threw punch after punch, but Faraj was far too skilled for any of them to land.

The soldier ducked another swing and punched the man in the right hip, forcing him to take several steps back toward the edge of the porch, which was exactly where Faraj wanted him.

The Queen's Guard's eyes flashed blue as his opponent once again ran for him. Faraj moved quickly and placed one steady foot forward in a lunge position as he tucked both fists against his chest. The moment the man stepped into range, Faraj thrust both fists outward, planting one in the man's chest and the other in his stomach. He cried out as Faraj's hard hits released a blast of power, throwing him onto the fertile earth in front of the house.

Power swelled in the air above Faraj, and his magic allowed him to feel the tiny vibrations traveling through the wood as the queen gracefully moved her body. The earth shook as a crevice opened before Faraj and swallowed his opponent up to the shoulders.

The wounded man on the porch let out a terrified gasp as he struggled to push himself away from Faraj. Looking to his left, the final two men on the porch stood staring at him, uncomfortably shifting their weight from one foot to the other as they debated what to do.

Faraj smiled. "Would you like to try with me, or would you like to run?" He extended a hand, inviting them to go as his smile grew. "But keep in mind..." his free hand moved to point above him, "I don't think you'll escape Queen Asim's reach. After all, isn't she *dangerous* and *paranoid*? I don't think she'll let you get too far."

"Oh, shit," the man bleeding out behind him muttered. It was quiet, but Faraj was able to hear it, which amused him greatly.

The remaining two who stood before him looked at one another with wide eyes, understanding the grave mistake they'd made.

Asim nearly laughed at Faraj's comment. She couldn't see the faces of whoever was left down there, but she could imagine they were priceless. Knowing her best guard could handle himself, she set her sights on the rest of the men she had heard around the side of the house earlier.

Coming to the edge of the porch roof, she saw that her men

were outnumbered, but only by a few. She took a deep breath, knowing that if she could even the playing field, her guards would pull through and win.

Every instinct in her body screamed for her to jump into the middle and defend her men and the innocent people inside the farmhouse. They were *her* people, and those men had come to prey on them.

Her brain, however, not so gently reminded her she wasn't *just* a warrior, she was a queen. She was a queen with thousands of innocent lives under her rule who looked to her for answers and strength. If she died and there was an attack by the beasts to the south, what would happen to her subjects?

She growled, hating the feeling of being so useless.

Taking a deep breath, she decided the best way to protect her men and herself was to cause a distraction.

Without further hesitation, Asim leapt off the porch roof, silently landing on the ground below. Looking to the left, she saw Faraj dealing with two men, who slowly lowered themselves to their knees and placed their hands behind their heads.

She was surprised they'd given themselves up, but then she'd opened the ground to bury a man up to his shoulders, which was a pretty powerful message.

Ducking, Asim reached out to touch the small rocks along the ground that were part of a path around the house. Her eyes flashed blue as her power flowed through her body.

Her hands balled into fists and tightened, crushing dozens of the small rocks into dust. The noise was muffled by the sounds of fighting in front of her, so she was free to move with little worry.

Her hands lifted, palms up, as she stood, the rock dust rising with her. Her graceful fingers danced as the dust mixed with the moisture she simultaneously pulled from the air around her. Thanks to the Nile, the farms and villages close to its banks had damper air than they had in the desert, and she was more than happy to use that to her advantage.

She thrust her hands forward, and the wet mixture whipped through the air and wrapped around the necks of two men closest to her. She then clenched her fists again, evaporating the water to harden the mixture. The men grabbed their throats, dropping their weapons to use both hands to pull on the rings.

Asim roughly yanked her hands back, pulling on the rings and taking the men to the ground. One of the rebels became visibly distracted by the noise and turned, allowing the guard opposing him to take control of the fight.

The guard knocked the man to the ground and punched him hard in the face, then grabbed a large stone and struck the man on the side of the head, knocking him unconscious. Asim wasn't sure if the rebel was dead or not, but given the deep, oozing wounds she saw on her guard's shoulder and the bare section of his chest, she didn't really care.

"Go, my Queen," her guard said as he stood. "Don't risk yourself."

"I'm not useless," she said, knowing he was right but wanting to help anyway.

He shook his head. "No, you're not. But if you die here, you *will* be. There's a war coming, and this isn't the battle we need you for."

Her eyes widened at his harsh and blunt words, not because they'd angered her but because they were true. Putting her pride away, she clenched her jaw in annoyance and took several steps back.

Wasting no time, the guard rushed back into the fight. Though she hated to do it, she stayed back to keep an eye on the three men on the ground. The first two still fought the rings around their necks, but they'd managed to climb to their feet.

"You bitch!" one shouted. "What did you do?"

"While I'd *love* to say, 'that's Queen Bitch to you,' I won't do the Great Queen a disservice. You should, however, close your mouth before I do far worse."

He spat on the ground, his face scrunching as he pulled hard on the ring again. "Fuck you. You're no queen of mine, and neither is that bitch in the sky. She's the reason all this is happening."

Asim smiled. "Well, this was a fun talk. Goodnight."

He opened his mouth to protest, but she flicked her wrist, and the ring threw the man toward the house. His head hit the side with a loud *thud*, and he fell to the ground, unconscious.

She looked at the other man with the ring around his neck. "What about you? Will you be a big boy and be nice, or do you need a nap, too?"

He shook his head and slowly sat down. "No trouble here. I know when I'm beaten."

Asim gave a curt nod. "Thank you. Put your hands behind your back, and I'll remove the ring around your throat."

He quickly did as she asked, and she went to work fashioning him stone handcuffs, a tight ring around each wrist with a three-inch-wide middle section to hold them together. Once his arms were secure, she closed her fist and crushed the one around his neck.

He took a deep breath and calmly said, "Thank you."

"No problem," she said as she secured the legs and wrists of the other two men on the ground.

The fighting died down faster than she'd thought it would. While her assistance hadn't truly been required, her taking out two had made it easier for the others to do what they needed to by focusing on only a single opponent. She wouldn't complain about that.

Two of her men had been seriously injured and the others had suffered minor injuries and broken bones. It could have been worse, and she knew that. Four of the rebels had died, three had serious injuries that might result in death, and the others would be fine.

They had plenty of people to question, and she planned to do just that. She'd need everyone to return with her to the city to guard the prisoners, but she planned to send soldiers back to check on the family and stay with them for a few days. Zuri wasn't among the men, and that was enough to make a pit form in her belly.

CHAPTER ELEVEN

Arryn and Corrine had been asleep and cuddled up together for nearly two days. They woke only long enough to drink, take a few bites of food, and use the bathroom, then they passed out again. When Arryn awoke on the third day, she felt better than ever.

Cathillian, Arryn called mentally.

Oh, look who's awake! Have you returned from the dead, or is this just a brief reprieve from your death sentence? he responded.

She smiled. *I think I'm awake. Is it day or night? I can't tell down here in the dungeon.*

It's midday. Corrine came up a few hours ago. Seems you two have a lot in common.

She yawned and sat up, stretching her achy body. She needed food and a lot of it if she hoped to feel more like herself again.

Get out here and get some food. Amon made all of us big-ass steaks!

Her eyes widened as her belly growled. "Don't have to tell me twice," she said to herself.

As Arryn stood, a bright light flashed in the room. She gasped when she saw a blood-red demon standing in front of her, its jaws wide open to reveal razor-sharp teeth. It snapped at her, and she dropped to the floor.

Her eyes flashed black as she scooted back several feet and arced her hands over her chest. She shuffled up to her knees, ready to throw the fireballs in her hands when she realized there was nothing to attack.

The flames illuminated a room that was devoid of any living creature other than her, but she spotted the switch across the room to activate the magitech lighting. She extinguished one of the fireballs as she stood on shaky legs to cross the room. As soon as the lights came on and she could see she was in no danger, she extinguished the other fireball.

What the hell was that? she wondered as she placed a hand on the wall to steady herself.

That was a glimpse of what you'll face when you reach your destination. Margit's harsh warning flowed through Arryn's mind, and she realized she hadn't checked in with the mystic in several days because of her magically induced coma. *What happened?*

Arryn's stomach growled, and she groaned in response. She wanted food, but she also needed to update Margit. It appeared the old woman was quite concerned for her well-being, not that she could blame her. Grown men didn't scare Arryn, but that thing had made her whole body tremble. She hadn't realized how terrified she was until then.

Opening her mind, Arryn sent a stream of images Margit's way, filling her in on what had happened since she'd last checked in. She could feel the mystic's disappointment through the connection.

Child, you're going to get yourself killed at this rate.

Arryn sighed. *Trust me, I figured that out. I've had a lot of close calls, but I always managed to pull out of them just fine. That one was a little too close, though. It was different somehow, even though I feel like I've seen worse. I wasn't myself.*

There was a pause before Margit replied, *That's not how you want to start the biggest journey of your life—with doubt. You're strong. Very strong, but that doesn't mean you're invincible. You need to stop taking unnecessary risks. Start assessing situations better. It will allow you to use less magic and conserve your energy.*

Flashes of what Margit had shown her whirled through her mind again. She realized that in all the times she'd fought before, it had been her survival instincts urging her on. Everything had been different back then. Now, those survival instincts urged her to run, but that wasn't an option. Running was never an option.

Believe me when I say I got a heaping helping of humility after that fight. Unfortunately, like you just said, it's made me unsteady. I'm in a new world with new people, surrounded by new versions of magic, and about to fight something I've never seen or heard of before. I'm worried I won't be enough.

Even across the connection, Arryn could hear a sigh from the old woman. *You won't be alone. More will come. You'll have help, and I think you'll find yourself capable of much more by the time you get out of all this. Just remember to meditate every day. Stop slacking. That little trick on the beach was pulled straight from your ass out of fear.*

Arryn nodded to herself. *I don't think I could recreate it if I tried. Speaking of which, how the hell did you create an illusion in my room this far away?*

A dry laugh echoed in Arryn's mind. *That was no illusion. Your mental barriers were down even before you let me all the way in. It wasn't hard for me to plant a strong image in your mind. Think of it more as a hallucination than an illusion.*

Well, I need to learn that one, Arryn responded.

You will in time. IF. YOU. PRACTICE!

Arryn smiled. *Okay, okay! I got it. I'm starving. I need to eat something and check on Corrine and the others, then I'll meditate. Does that appease the queen?*

The mental image of Margit rolling her eyes and shaking her head as she heavily sighed fluttered through Arryn's mind. *I'm no queen, child. You, however, are a royal pain in my ass.*

Arryn laughed. *Well, I try.*

Unfortunately, you succeed. Often. Now go eat. I expect you to check in before nightfall.

Yes, ma'am, Arryn said before closing the connection and putting up her mental barrier.

She took a deep breath and slowly blew it out, steadying herself. Though it had been a few minutes, the mental image of what she'd seen still haunted her.

More will come. Those words echoed in her mind. Did the old woman know something she didn't or had she meant Arryn would find help once they arrived in Kemet? With most people, she wouldn't have even thought about it, but with Margit, she could never be too sure.

After going to the main room, Arryn was seated at a reserved table with a large steak waiting for her. It was medium, just how she liked it, and came with mashed potatoes and green veggies. Her mouth had started watering the instant she'd smelled it, and the taste was even better than she'd imagined. At that moment, she was certain this was the place Mariana had talked about.

Once her belly was full, she made her way to the bar, where Amon put down a tray of drinks for one of the girls to take to her waiting tables.

"Thank you for lunch. That was the best steak I've ever had, but if you ever go to the Dark Forest, don't tell the Chieftain I said that."

He laughed, the sound deep and rich. "You got it. I'm glad you liked it. How are you feeling?"

She nodded. "I'm better. Much better. I can't believe how quiet it is down in our room. I assumed that with a bar here, it would be noisy as hell."

"That was a neat trick. When I built this place, I hired Kemetian builders from the city. They're much different than builders anywhere else. The building above the ground is all wood. I couldn't reinforce the upper floors and make them soundproof because of the added weight, so I decided to put the brothel up there. Downstairs, however, it's well insulated with concrete created by Jadid builders. It's quiet enough we could have secluded rooms down there for our more...*innocent* guests."

The more she heard about the Kemetian people, the more excited she was to meet them. Though they were already in Kemet, Jadid was the heart of it. From what she could tell, the people in the city were like the people of the Dark Forest—well-trained, each specializing in a specific task and using it to benefit the community and help it flourish and grow.

"It worked. Money well spent, I'd say," she replied. "Speaking of, when would you like us to take care of your friend's child? I'd say we've racked up quite a bill for two days' stay with room and board, stables, meals, and anything else you've provided."

He smiled. "Your friend Cathillian has helped some. Small healing sessions. I told him not to tire himself. The boy looks much better, and he's able to eat again, which was his mother's biggest worry. Why don't you take a few minutes to acclimate and get used to being back among the living?" He winked. "Once you're ready, I'll take you to them."

She was grateful for his kindness. Not only had he cared for all of them and gave them shelter and safety, but he was also very patient. Most people would see their fatigue and make demands in such a situation. While she didn't like sitting around while a child suffered, she knew healing him too quickly could cause adjustment changes and do harm too. Chronic illnesses were *nothing* like acute issues.

"Thank you for being so kind and patient. I appreciate it. I would like to see my friends. Where are they?"

He pointed toward the kitchen. "They went out back. The young one wanted to train."

Arryn rolled her eyes. "Of course, she did. She's been awake for a few hours after being in a magical coma for days, and the first thing she wants to do is push herself."

The man smiled and shrugged. "She's strong. Resilient. She wants to be like her adopted mother. Kids bounce back easier than we do. You're what, twenty-three?"

"Close. Twenty."

He nodded. "Even as young as you are, that energy is gone. If you let her push herself, let her go as hard as she chooses, there's no telling what she'll be capable of."

"I think you're right about that," she said. "Though, if I'm any proof, going too hard for too long can wear you down to the point you have a tough time getting back up."

She often wondered what would have happened if her learning hadn't been stunted when she was Corrine's age. It was true that she'd had a hard time with magic when she was younger, but had she been able to attend the academy and continue training with her mother, she might have been much more powerful.

Then again, it was possible she might have been weaker for it. Without her mother's death and the belief that her father was dead, too, she might never have realized her potential.

If she could help it, she would never make Corrine ask herself that question.

"Duty calls," Amon said, pointing to a patron. "If you head through the kitchen, you'll find a door leading out back. That's where they'll be."

"Thank you," she said, offering a quick smile before making her way through the building.

The group was much calmer than they had been when she first arrived, and she was happy about that. She didn't like Corrine seeing the women and the behavior of the rude men in there, but she reminded herself it was her Arcadian side telling her that.

Truth was, in the Dark Forest, there was no shame. Sex wasn't a forbidden topic. Arryn remembered overhearing a rather adult conversation shortly after arriving there. She'd been embarrassed, but then curiosity had gotten the best of her.

She'd repeated what she'd heard to Cathillian, and he'd told her in detail what they'd meant. He hadn't been much older than her, but to him, it was no big deal. Everything in the Dark Forest was relaxed, and no one batted an eye if they walked in on someone bathing or changing. The body was considered natural. Seeing a breast was no different from seeing an arm.

In Arcadia, however, things were much different. Unless they came from people from the Boulevard or drunks at a bar, sexual comments and topics were considered rude and uncivilized. That wasn't to say they weren't heard, but Arcadians were far more prudish than druids.

Most of the time, Arryn didn't care, but when it came to Corrine, sometimes an overprotective Arcadian mother came to the front instead of a druid.

Arryn smiled as she looked left out the back door. The stables sat sixty or more feet behind the establishment. The horses were drinking water from a large trough, the tigers lying in the sun not far away. Cathillian laid on the ground with his back against Dante. He was shirtless, with his arms under his head and his eyes closed.

While she could feel the intense heat where she stood in the shade, as she took a few steps closer, she noticed at least a fifteen-degree decrease in temperature. Cathillian was controlling the temperature in their area with little effort as he rested. She sometimes forgot how powerful he was.

Farther to the left, she saw Bast, Cleo, and Corrine. They had their backs to Arryn, so she was able to watch without being seen. Each of them stood in a similar position: feet wider than shoulder-width apart, squatting with their arms in front of them. Their arms swayed like thin branches on a tree in the wind. Gently and methodically, they moved to their left and then to their right. It looked like a dance.

Bast and Cleo stepped back, but they urged Corrine to continue. Arryn watched with interest as the young girl continued to sway. Her movements became smoother and more agile. Soon, she saw the sand at the girl's feet swish back and forth.

"Keep going!" Bast encouraged. "You're doing it!"

Arryn could feel Corrine beaming from there. The little girl had learned so much and was driven to learn even more. She seemed infinitely older than she was. Thinking about it, she wasn't sure when Corrine's birthday was. From what she knew of Corrine's life, she wondered if the girl even knew.

Without warning, Corrine screeched when she got too carried away and a small wall of sand was thrown at the stables. Cleo was quick to stop it, stomping a foot forward and throwing a flat hand directly out in front of her. The sand looked as though it hit an invisible wall as it stopped hard and fell to the ground.

Arryn looked down and reached outward with her nature magic, but she felt nothing. There was no connection with the sand. She wondered if the twins used telekinesis to move the sand or if it was something else.

She was able to move sand with physical magic, but it was clunky and not controlled like with the twins' magic. She'd always assumed they'd used an altered form of physical magic, but maybe they had some kind of connection with sand and rock like she did with plants.

"Arryn!" Corrine called before running at full speed toward her.

The druid smiled and absorbed the impact, hugging her tight. "Hey, tiny. I'm glad you're feeling better!"

"I am! I've missed you! I'm glad you're feeling better, too. Did you see what I just did? It was good, right? Well, until I accidentally almost hurt the horses."

Arryn laughed. "I saw. You did a *great* job." She looked at

Cathillian, who hadn't moved. She reached out mentally and realized he'd fallen asleep in the short time since she'd spoken to him.

She sighed. "You're lucky I'm still waking up," she said to his sleeping form.

Corrine laughed. "You want to mess with him, don't you?"

Arryn nodded. "It feels like forever since I've played a good joke on him. One day... One day *soon*."

CHAPTER TWELVE

Asim hadn't slept well after everything that had happened. She'd been so focused on the potential threat down south that she hadn't thought of anything more domestic.

By the time they'd returned, she was exhausted, and so were the others. She'd sent rested soldiers as messengers to the other two locations to retrieve the others while she and the guards who'd accompanied her got some much-needed rest.

When she awoke, she headed to the jail instead of going down to get breakfast as she normally would before going back to work in the tunnels. Upon arriving, she saw Faraj and Shai were already there, standing guard and waiting for their queen.

Asim gave each of them a nod of acknowledgment. "Good morning. Have you spoken to our prisoners?"

Shai shook his head. "No, Your Highness. We wanted to wait for you so you could hear with your own ears."

"There's something you should know before going down there," Faraj said. She looked at him curiously, and he continued, "One of them, the one you said surrendered to you? He's originally from Jadid. He's the clothing merchant you used to take the princesses to see."

Her eyes widened. "What? Nafari?"

Faraj nodded. "Yes. While I didn't ask him anything I thought you might want to hear an answer to, I did verify it was him. It seems he left here out of fear of the monsters to the south."

She shook her head. "I don't understand that logic. I've heard people are worried a larger group makes for a larger target, but I have to believe we're safer in numbers, especially with all the magic users in the city."

"Their way of thinking is strong. Perhaps we should talk to him and get his side. Maybe he can make things clearer for us," Shai suggested.

Asim sighed. "I suppose you're right."

She extended her hand, inviting them to show her to the prisoners. They made their way through the large stone building toward the back, then walked through a door on the right and down a flight of steps down to the cells. Asim turned a corner and went into a separate room that was used for questioning.

She didn't have to wait long before Faraj and Shai brought Nafari in. The moment she saw his face in the magitech lighting, she recognized him. Even with a half-moon, while in the shadow of the house, she hadn't been able to make out his facial features the night before. Thinking back, she recalled how familiar his voice had sounded.

"Why didn't you say anything?" Queen Asim asked as Nafari took a seat across the table from her.

He shrugged. "Shame, I suppose. It only took a couple of seconds to realize you had no idea who I was. I wasn't sure if that was because you'd forgotten me or if you couldn't recognize me in the darkness. Either way, I didn't want you to see me like that."

She scoffed. "That's interesting to hear."

"I suppose it is. I can't blame you for not believing me."

There was a pause as she peered into his eyes and searched his face. He seemed genuine to her, but she hadn't spoken to him enough yet to know if that was true.

"I don't know what to believe yet," she said, tapping a restless finger on the table. "What happened to you? You were the royal clothier and a friend to me and my girls—*your* princesses. I want to know why you left, but I'm more interested in how you ended up...*here*!" She gestured to the interrogation room. "Speak freely. I want to know everything."

"You can ask me anything, my Queen. I will answer to the best of my ability."

Asim let out an unamused laugh. "Am I? Am I still your queen?"

He nodded. "Yes. This might look bad, but I assure you, my loyalty never wavered. I'll explain."

She sat back in her chair and crossed her arms over her chest. It wasn't the most regal position, but she didn't feel the need to be perfect every moment of every day. She shared that trait with her daughters.

"When the portals first opened months ago, nothing came through. At least, no one witnessed anything. They were there for a week or two, maybe more, before anyone saw anything. The beasts were small, no larger than a small or medium-sized dog. They'd come through, sniff around, and then go back. Honestly, it didn't seem like much of a threat, though it was terrifying that a hole had been ripped in the world.

"As a clothier, I made things for the very poor all the way to up to the throne. I never allowed my association with you and the princesses to make me feel entitled or better than anyone else. I was what I was, and that was that. As such, I had travelers, farmers, wanderers, and everyone in between come across my stand. I heard stories."

"What kind of stories?" the queen asked. "About the portals?"

He nodded. "Yes. People flocked to see it. It was a long tear through our world, and they said it looked like it was bleeding with how red it was. Who wouldn't be curious?" He waited for a moment, but Asim said nothing, so he continued. "I too grew curious, and I went to see it for myself. When I tell you that was the most horrifying thing I've ever seen, trust me that it's an understatement. Seeing something like that...it changes you."

"Changes you how? It makes you turn your back on a long-time friend? On the crown? The *people*?" Asim demanded, her voice growing louder with every question.

"No, Your Highness. It terrified me. I became far more afraid of what might come through that thing than of any man, and two days later, something the size of a horse came through and ripped a large group of people apart. When I heard that, my fear grew. I had this inescapable terror that something bad was going to happen.

"There were some who said they believed it was a hell portal. The old religions have been lost and forgotten by most, but those who still believed thought it was the gates of hell opening to release the apocalypse on us. Others..." He paused.

Her eyes narrowed. "Others what? What do the others believe?"

Nafari took a deep breath and slowly blew it out. She could hear a quiver in it and knew he was afraid.

"The attacks after that were random and came slowly at first. A couple weeks between them, give or take. It seemed the smaller beasts that came through were scouts, checking out the area to report back to the larger ones. When they came through, they hit one village, then another, and another. Within a month, they had cleared out a five-mile radius."

"That doesn't answer the question, Nafari," she said, impatience leaking into her voice.

He nodded. "I know. I'm getting there."

"Good. Perhaps you should hurry because I know these stories, too. It's why I'm working my ass off to protect the city—the same city you and your new friends seem hell-bent on sacking. So please, continue. *Quickly*."

He swallowed hard and nodded. "As you know, it's not like

anyone could get close enough to the monsters to study them. The only thing anyone had to go on was behavior. What they'd learned was that large groups were a magnet for them. People were *convinced* of that, and even the most intelligent of us who have studied animals believed it. To me, that was proof enough.

"I packed my things and got the hell out of Jadid. If they were attracted to larger groups of people, I didn't want to be anywhere near here. It seemed everyone would be safer if they split up. As I traveled, trying to find a little place to carve out for myself where I could continue my business, I met people who had done the same. That's how I met Zuri."

"Zuri. That's the man we've heard so much about?" Asim asked.

Nafari nodded. "If you've heard about him, I assume so. Charismatic? Persuasive?"

She nodded. "He is the one, yes. No one we've spoken to is afraid of him. Those who would speak said good things, but some have had bad feelings about him, regardless of how nice he seemed."

Nafari nodded again, placing his hands flat on the table and staring at them for a moment before continuing.

"There's a good reason for that. He's an *excellent* actor. A manipulator. He'll say, do, or act any way he must to achieve his goal. To twist people into doing what he wants. When I first met him, he came off as very driven. He seemed stubborn, but not in a bad way. He had a goal in mind—safety and security for the country, or so he'd have anyone believe—so I didn't question it. Not at first.

"I've met some of your soldiers and personal Queen's Guard, and they give off that same energy. I was used to it, so I overlooked it. He said he believed, much as I and many others did, that smaller groups equaled a better chance of survival. They also believed the portals weren't from hell."

"Then where *did* they think they came from?" Shai asked before Asim could.

"They think the Matriarch and Patriarch are behind this," Nafari stated flatly. Asim could see the disbelief in his expression. He found it to be just as ridiculous as she did.

"They think...*the Queen* is behind all this?"

Nafari nodded. "Yes. They think she's been watching the world from the stars and is angry at what she sees. They think she's opened portals to another world to send those demons in to start the apocalypse."

Asim's eyes widened. "The apocalypse? Started by Bethany Anne? Are they insane?"

She thought for a moment, remembering back to when the man she'd fought called her a bitch. She'd told him she'd like to say, "That's Queen Bitch to you," but she didn't want to do the Great Queen a disservice. He'd told her Bethany Anne was the one responsible for all this.

"Now that I think about it, I recall your friend saying something about that. So, this Zuri fellow believes the Bitch and the Bastard have become fed up with the world, so they've begun the apocalypse? That they opened a portal to send wicked hellbeasts in to destroy us all for our wicked ways? He thinks *all* of that, yet his *oh-so-wise* decision to combat this is to lie, cheat, and steal his way to safety? Because *that's* going to redeem mankind?"

Nafari nodded. "They don't think of the Bitch as a goddess. They believe she existed, and they believe she was powerful, but they think she's just like anyone else who has too much power— corrupt and murderous."

Asim rolled her eyes. "Pot, kettle, I suppose. Hmm. I see. How interesting. Well, I don't give a damn if someone believes in her or doesn't or if they think she's a hero or destroyer of worlds. What they *will* do is leave innocent people alone."

"Sorry to butt in, but how did his crackpot theories shift into creating a whole fucking army to take down the crown?" Faraj snapped.

"I don't know the full truth. I doubt anyone knows except those closest to him. When I met him, he was obsessed with creating an army to protect the south from the demons. Like those people you mentioned earlier, I had this strange gut feeling, but he seemed like a great man who was deeply concerned about the people. I had no reason to doubt him at the time.

"Zuri believed that living in as small of a group as possible was important, but that we should still have an army in case the worst happened. After all, we were outside the protection of the city walls, and the soldiers were gone for the time being. While we believed Jadid was doomed to get hit, we also knew the thick walls created an exceptionally good barrier. Anyone in the city stood a better chance than we did while out in the open.

"At first, I helped Zuri travel around to different farms, to small villages, and to lonely houses along the river to recruit men who would be willing to fight the monsters if they moved north. We grew the army to several hundred in just two weeks, and we had a plan in place in case the demons came too close. It allowed everyone to stay separated until the time came, then soldiers would gather while word spread of the danger.

"Every location had messengers designated to ride as fast as possible to the next to get help. It wasn't perfect, but it was there. Last night, though..." He stopped, his brows furrowing as he shook his head. "That was something else. That was the first time I'd heard that story."

"You expect me to believe he changed from noble protector to traitor overnight?" Asim asked.

Nafari shook his head. "It wasn't overnight. Like I said, I had no reason to doubt him *in the beginning*. Over time, I overheard a random loud statement from one of those he trusted most, or I saw the anger in his eyes, or I saw him speak to someone and noticed tell-tale signs of him trying to control himself, something an honest man doesn't need to do in casual conversation.

"The man, the *illusion*, dissipated when I saw how hard he had to work to keep himself from boiling over. Those he spoke to seemed oblivious, but sitting back and watching, it was pretty obvious. I hated that I not noticed before. For the last week or two, he had seemed to be on edge, ready for a fight. I wasn't in on his private conversations, but I'd heard rumors he might want to take the city. I just didn't believe it until last night."

"Why didn't he go with you? Did he know we would be there?" Shai asked.

He turned his head enough to the left so he could look at Shai. "As far as I know, no. He sent us because he had planning to do. Well, that's what he said anyway. If I'm honest, I think it was because he was losing control and knew he wouldn't be able to keep his true nature from coming out. He wanted to achieve his goals, and it was obvious he wanted to skip the pleasantries and the façade and just threaten people into joining him. It would have been easier, especially with his numbers, but it wouldn't have created *loyalty*. He needed that."

Shai nodded. "Yeah. And if word spread that he'd threatened them into joining him, those he'd convinced he was a good man with a noble cause would have been lost. They'd have turned on him. Not to mention, if a war with the city *did* break out, any who'd been threatened into joining him would have no reason to stick around. They would turn tail and join us."

"Sounds like even though he was losing control, he still had common sense," Asim said. "His choice to send the other man, who was less invested and therefore more likely to keep his cool, was wise."

Nafari turned back to face the queen. "I'm so sorry. I had a bad feeling, but I didn't realize the plan had come to that. There were so many secret meetings and whispers. He has a core group he keeps close, and I suspect it's because those men are just like him. The rest of us are pawns, and no one has realized it. That was why I surrendered. I didn't want to fight, especially when I realized it was the royal guard we were up against. I knew it was wrong, but part of me worried at least some of the men I was with were as unaware as I was."

"Judging by how dedicated they are to your man Zuri, I'd have to say that's a big fucking no," Faraj said. He sighed. "Or I suppose you could be right. It's unsurprising a charismatic man could take control of a large number of people by using their fears against them while offering a friendly smile and the promise of hope."

Nafari faced Faraj. "I didn't see anyone else in the cells. Was there a man with light brown skin and green eyes? He had braids he kept tied up high, and the hair on the sides and back of his head was shaved off."

"No," Faraj. "He wasn't among the living. He was one of the bodies we buried east of the farm."

Nafari's eyes widened. "Oh, no."

"What?" Asim asked roughly.

"That was Zuri's only son. He was everything to him. Whatever plans he had against you before—" Nafari shook his head, obvious concern showing in his sad eyes, "I worry that was only the beginning. If he finds out the royal guard killed his son, he will stop at nothing to come for the city."

Asim sighed, knowing this was only the beginning. Things were about to get much worse. She stood and stared down at the table. "My daughters can't get back here soon enough. Let's hope the rumors about the people from the magical Valley are true." She locked eyes with Nafari. "Thank you for your honesty. I have to think about this, so for now, you're going back to your cell."

"For *now*?" Faraj asked. "Forgive me, my Queen, but what does that mean?"

"I need to think. That's what it means." Her voice had a tone that strongly suggested the conversation was over. Faraj took the hint and nodded, allowing her to pass without further questions.

CHAPTER THIRTEEN

Z uri sat outside by a large fire he'd started with his physical magic. His men kept their distance, but he could hear them whispering. He only allowed those closest to him to surround him at night or if he was in a bad mood. If he needed to speak to anyone or make plans in a hurry, he didn't want outsiders around. The image he'd created was everything, and he wouldn't risk that for any reason. Especially now.

His eyes, still coal-black, stared with utter hatred into the flames.

Initially, he hadn't worried when his crew hadn't returned. He'd told his son to go, and his son knew better than anyone what he wanted to achieve. He *understood* what Zuri wanted to achieve. He trusted his son implicitly to carry out his orders, and he hadn't expected anything bad to happen.

It was nearly four the following afternoon when he became worried. Zuri hurried to gather a search party and headed toward the farm he'd ordered them to visit.

When they'd arrived earlier that evening, they found only a farmer and his wife and their thirteen-year-old daughter. Rage fueled him, but he forced himself to remain as calm as possible. He wanted answers. Either his son was off doing who knew what or something bad had happened. One way or another, Zuri would figure it out.

The farmer had been kind at first, but it didn't take long for him to start squirming as the questions became more detailed. It was obvious he knew more than he was letting on, and *nothing* pissed Zuri off more than being lied to or stolen from.

"Zuri," one of his men said, daring to speak his name.

The feared leader slowly turned his head, his eyes focusing on the man who'd torn him from his thoughts. "*What?*" he ground out.

"I-I'm sorry, boss. It's just, we'd like to do something to help. Anything."

Zuri stared at him for several moments before glancing at the ground to his right, where his murdered son's corpse lay, wrapped and ready for a proper burial.

His throat tightened as tears stung his eyes. He cleared his throat and sniffed once before putting on his stony expression again. "The brat. Tell Asher to bring her."

The men scurried off to do as he'd asked without hesitation.

"*Please! We didn't do anything wrong,*" the farmer had said, pleading on his knees for Zuri not to end them, but it was too late.

He'd sent three of his men off to look around after he saw blood spatter and other signs of a struggle around the farmhouse. Within thirty or so minutes, one of his men returned with the news they'd found several shallow graves, and his son was among them.

"*Didn't do anything wrong?*" he'd asked the farmer. "*You killed my son! You took him from me!*"

The man had continued to plead for his family, but it would do him no good. A young teenage girl fought past her mother to run out the door to help her father just then.

"Leave him alone!" she'd shouted at him. So strong. So fearless.

Movement out of the corner of his eye pulled him back to the present again when Asher returned with the girl. Her wrists were tied, and he gave her a light shove every few feet, but she remained quiet. That face, though... Zuri smiled. The rage on her face hadn't left since he'd killed her parents and taken her with his group.

"Well, if I didn't know any better, I'd say you didn't much care for me," Zuri said.

"No shit," she said and spat on the ground at his feet.

"A little young to use that language, aren't you? Oh, wait, there's no one to get after you for it now, is there?" He laughed as she growled.

"I don't know how yet, but I'm going to kill you for what you did."

Zuri shrugged and sat back in his chair. "Even if it was just you and me, kid, you wouldn't stand a chance. Good fucking luck with all of us. You're just going to have to bide your time until I figure out what to do with you."

"Why did you take me?" she asked.

His eyes narrowed, and he stood. "You're too young to understand, but you're gonna learn today."

He roughly grabbed her by the arm and pulled her toward him as he walked over to his son's body.

"Your father did this. This is *my* son. He's dead because of what your spineless father did. Because of his weakness, his *stupidity*, my son is dead. Your father took my son, so I took his daughter. We're even."

She turned, rage in her teary eyes. "Then kill me! This isn't even! You killed *them* and left *me* alive! This isn't even close."

He took a step forward, lowering his face to hers. "Be careful what you wish for. If I kill you now, how will you get your revenge later?"

The girl's eyes narrowed as a dark smile crossed her lips. "You're absolutely right. Thanks for reminding me."

"Good girl," he said as he straightened and patted her on the head. "Now, unless you want to know how it feels to be thrown into a fire, I suggest you talk. Who killed my son? It sure as shit wasn't your cowardly father."

Her nostrils flared when he mentioned her father, but she managed to keep calm. "I didn't know them. Royal, that's all I know. I've never been to Jadid, but I know the uniform."

Zuri stopped and thought for a moment about the scene. There had been a large crack in the ground in front of the house, nearly twenty feet in length. The ground had been broken apart and resealed, and there was a filled-in hole. It was flush with the rest of the ground, but it was obvious it had been recently disturbed.

He sighed. "Of course. City magic users."

"Am I free to go back to bed?" she asked sternly.

"What's your name, girl?" Zuri asked.

She hesitated for several moments. "Amara."

"Good to know. You can go. Just remember, you're still here because I don't know what to do with you yet. Death isn't off the table, especially if you piss me off or annoy me. Got it?"

"Yup. Got it."

He smiled and shook his head at the level of disdain in her voice. He had to give it to her, though, she'd managed to control her temper quite well. She was a lot better at it than he was.

With a wave, Asher handed the girl off to someone who would take her back to her sleeping quarters. He'd threatened the lives of everyone there not to lay a hand on her, so he was fairly certain no one would.

"What are you going to do?" Asher asked. "We can't let this stand. Those were soldiers, maybe even the queen's personal guard. If they've found out about us…"

Zuri nodded. "We risk word spreading. I know. Trust me, I'm not going to let that bitch get the upper hand." He sighed heavily before looking at Asher. "I think we need to kick this up a notch. Those otherworld demons from the bitch queen attacked again. They're coming farther north, and we can't risk it. We're two or more days' ride away, but I still don't trust it. We need more people."

Asher shook his head. "Word has spread about the desert king rising. It's obviously reached the queen, or they wouldn't have come looking for you. Your plan has worked so far. You have everyone right where you want them, an army ready to do whatever you want. The more people you 'save,' the more loyal they grow. Others who are indifferent are on their own because they know the monsters attack larger groups. They're the tricky ones. Why the hell would they want to join a growing army if that would make them a target?"

Zuri smiled. "Because we still have a lot of distance between us and the monsters—for now. That will change if the most recent attack is any indication. As for the rest, they might be hesitant, but it's not set in stone. They just need a damn good reason."

"What's that supposed to mean? Do you have a grand plan you'd like to share with the rest of the class?"

"Of course!" Zuri snapped his fingers.

A young woman rushed over with a cup and pitcher. She poured him a cup of ale and bowed her head slightly before turning away.

He took several gulps before sighing heavily. "What if we found one of those monsters? Caught it?"

Asher's eyes widened. "Are you fucking insane? Weren't you *just* saying how safe we were because of our distance? Why the hell would you want to go find one?"

"Think about it. We catch one and put it in one of those big-game cages. We use it as bait. These villages have spread out—no more than a hundred people in a settlement now. Most are no more than fifty. If we take the horses out there with one of those bastards on a wagon and poke it, I bet it'll scream. We'll be way too far away from the other demons for them to hear and come to the rescue, but the people in the villages will hear."

"So, you're planning to scare the shit out of them?" Asher asked. "All due respect, friend, but I think your grief is clouding your judgment."

Zuri nodded. " I think you're wrong about that. It has to be more than scaring them. See, they'll send their patrol out to check out the situation. When they come, we'll make it look realistic. Kill 'em, gut 'em like a wild animal would, and leave the parts for the villagers to find. They'll be so sure the monsters have come for them that they'll be begging to join us."

"That's pretty fucking cold even for you, man," Asher said. "You think it'll work? I mean, think about it. Catching one of those things…" He shook his head. "That sounds like a death sentence."

"We only have to pull this off once. If we do, word will spread of an attack this far north of the portal, and the villagers, farmers, and everyone in between will seek us out."

Asher huffed a sarcastic laugh. "Yeah, and so will the *queen*! You remember her? The bitch who figured us out?"

Zuri shrugged. "Won't matter. By then, we'll have the army we need. We'll be ready. Not to mention, if we keep that thing alive, we could let it loose on them. I've always wanted to take that damned city, not that I ever thought I'd get a chance. Now, I have no choice. I *will* have revenge for what they did to my boy."

Asher took a deep breath and sighed heavily. "I'm gonna take a wild guess and say you can't be talked out of this, right?"

"Exactly. I'm *positive* this will work. The plans may vary a bit, depending on the situation. Shit changes in the field, everyone knows that. You just have to trust me."

After several moments of hesitation, Asher groaned and rolled his eyes. "Fine, but this better not get us killed. You might be the one in charge, but you made me your right hand for a reason. I'm the person who helps you not end up dead."

Zuri smiled. "Good. Glad to have you on board."

CHAPTER FOURTEEN

Arryn and her group spent a total of four days at Amon's establishment. Each day, they gave slow-acting healings to the young boy who had been afflicted with something the druids identified as a severe form of degenerative muscular disease. Cathillian healed him in the morning, Arryn healed him after lunch, and Corrine, the best healer among them, gave him a heavy healing in the evening right before bed.

Over the course of several days, his muscles filled back out and he was able to stand, though he would need physical therapy to learn how to walk properly again. Arryn knew it was only a temporary fix, just like any chronic illness with no cure was. Without their help, he would have lived no more than between thirteen and sixteen years, but they'd given him another five years at least.

That meant every three to five years, his mother would have to travel to the Dark Forest or find healers who were closer that could do healings at that level. Arryn thought of the young Daoine boy she'd met. After he matured and learned how to control his healing abilities, he would be a good candidate, but she didn't think he'd be ready for several years after the ailing boy would need him. After all, he had no one to teach him.

After finishing on their mid-day healing on the fourth day, they decided it was time to go. They'd upheld their end of the bargain, and they didn't want to take any more resources from Amon unpaid.

To Arryn's surprise, as they loaded their gear onto the horses, and each of them climbed onto their respective mounts, Amon rounded the corner of his building with a two-horse wagon.

Arryn smiled. "Where are you going?"

He returned the smile. "I'm going with you to the capital. I think I can help you."

"Help us?" Arryn asked. "What about your business? You're leaving everything behind?"

Amon nodded. "Now that my friend's son is healed, she and the other girls will look out for business. I've left it in their hands for a few days before, and I haven't been disappointed. Besides, I've never been to the capital, and you could use the extra hands. I assure you I'm a skilled fighter, and I know how to use my magic well."

"He's not wrong," Cathillian said. "We could use the help. We can use anything we can get, and we've seen him drop a man with hardly any effort."

"Aye, lassie. Little Zoe was quite the force ta be reckoned with, an' he's a lot bigger. We should let 'im come if 'e wants ta," Samuel added.

She sighed and looked at Amon as Margit's words fluttered through her mind. The old woman had mentioned more would join her, and this made her wonder if the woman was more psychic than she let on.

"Do you understand what we're going to do?" Arryn asked.

Amon nodded. "I've heard the stories, and I've seen the images on the surface of your thoughts." Her brows rose as she looked at him with borderline anger. He smiled. "You project your thoughts when you're worried. Your barrier fails, and the images are right on the surface. I never peeked, but as a mental magic user, I couldn't avoid them. Kind of like talking to someone within earshot but not in the conversation. They may not *want* to hear it, but they can't help what their ears pick up."

That was a clear enough answer for her. She sensed no ill intentions from him, and even Margit had told Arryn how shitty her mental barriers were. She needed to work on them, and having Amon around would be an excellent way to practice.

She nodded. "Okay. Well, if you've seen the images, then you know we're up against some terrifying monsters. I don't know what they are or where they came from, but it's our job to kick their asses and hopefully figure out how to close the portals."

"I'm in." Without waiting for anyone to say anything else, he flicked the reins, urging his horses forward.

"What's in the wagon?" Cleo asked as she rode next to him on her horse. "Too good to camp out on the ground?"

Amon laughed. "Not hardly. This wagon is full of barrels of mystic's brew and some of the finest wine in the area."

"Hey, hey, hey!" Samuel said, riding quickly to catch up to Amon on the other side of the wagon. "Did ye say ye have *mystic's brew*? How the hell did ye get any o' that?" He paused. "Wait! Why the hell didn't ye offer it?"

"I had no idea any of you knew what it was, and I save it for myself, my employees, and those who pay the best."

"Where the *hell* do ye think that shite came from, laddie? The Heights and Craigston! Where I come from!"

"Easy there, Samuel. You're getting worked up over nothing," Cathillian said, smiling at the rearick.

"I'm sorry," Amon said. "I had no idea. I've never seen your kind before, so I had no way of knowing. I apologize for not offering you some. Given all you'd done for my friend, I should have. I apologize for my rudeness."

"It's no big deal," Arryn said. "He's just crabby because he misses home and we dragged him across the sea. If you've never met a rearick before, you should feel lucky he's the first."

Amon smiled as he watched ahead of him. "Yeah? Why's that?"

Arryn snorted. "Because that grumpy little ball of hair is the *least* bitter rearick I've ever met."

Everyone laughed except Samuel. "Ooh, Matriarch take you all. Lass, here I thought we were friends. Shows what I know."

Snow picked up speed to walk next to Samuel's horse. Arryn smiled at him. "You know you're family. Don't doubt it for a second."

The scowling rearick hid a smile. "Shut yer trap, woman."

Laughing, she said, "I love you, too."

"If you've never met a rearick, how do you get mystic's brew?" Cathillian asked Amon.

"When I was in my early teens, mystic missionaries traveled to my hometown and stayed for weeks. I had already discovered my use of mental magic, but I was the only one around who used that school. Everyone was mildly afraid of me, but I never understood why. Looking back, I understand, but I didn't then. It wasn't until those mystics came through and taught me some control and showed the town how fun it could be that everyone started to see me a bit different.

"Over the weeks, I trained day and night with them, and they taught me their brand of storytelling. Since they couldn't bring enough of the mystic's brew with them on their travels, they made a few barrels in each town they went to and shared it with the locals during storytime. We'd all gather in a bar or in the square, and they'd tell these grand stories about their travels, with beautiful images of places we'd never seen. Before they left, they taught me how to make the drink. They said I was one of them and I should know how, even if it wasn't strictly allowed."

"That's incredible," Arryn said. "Did you travel when you were old enough? That seems like the mystics' way of life. Everyone goes on some kind of journey."

He nodded. "I did. I traveled east and met some of the most incredible people. The farther east you go, the bigger the cultural differences are. I'm originally from a southern part of the continent, but when I arrived in Kemet, it was just home. I loved it here, so I stayed. I've been here for over a decade."

"And you never went to the capital?" Bast asked. "If you enjoy finding and learning about new cultures so much, why didn't you visit? It's rich there."

He shrugged. "I always planned to, but I started my business and got busy with that and never got a chance. All the traveling I've done since has been to acquire supplies or food for the inn. This is a new experience, and I assume we will meet the queen if we're going to the capital with plans to save it. I wanted to come bearing gifts."

"The alcohol is for m—"

"It's for the queen?" Cleo said, interrupting her sister.

"It is!" Amon said with excitement. "I've never met royalty. I was always taught that if you show up to another's home, especially without an invite, you offer a gift. I have nothing valuable a queen would want, but I do have a talent for making the brew and a large stock of aged wines."

Bast snorted, and Arryn saw Cleo shoot her a look of warning. Arryn was curious about the twins' strange behavior, but she let it go. She rode in silence, listening to the group ask Amon question after question about his many travels.

Kemet was far different than she'd imagined. After moving through the desert for a while, they traveled next to patches of fertile land that were close enough to the great river to flourish. There were many towns and villages, and everything amazed her. While the earth had healed, it was obvious to her that the landscape used to be much different.

After several hours of travel, they reached a bigger town, and she could see the evidence of old roads, buildings, and more. Off in the distance were larger, more rundown buildings, some of them giant, but those closer to the town were smaller. They had been partially restored and repurposed for stables and other things.

"What is all that?" Arryn asked. "I've never seen anything like it."

"We are nearing the remnants of an ancient city. Well, it was built by the new ancients," Bast said. "The closer to our home we get, the larger the buildings are. Some were hundreds of feet tall long ago, but time and war devastated the area. Over the centuries, Kemetians have torn down or repurposed some of those buildings. The steel that wasn't too damaged was used for weapons, or in some cases, was able to be turned into outbuildings like barns or stables."

"Buildings hundreds of feet tall, huh?" Arryn asked.

Cleo looked at her and smiled. "Just wait. You haven't seen anything yet."

Arryn smiled back, full of excitement. As afraid as she'd been, she was now full of wonder. Kemet was much more than she'd imagined, and every mile they traveled showed her something new and beautiful.

"I can't wait to see it!" she exclaimed.

Cleo nodded. "Most of the towns you see were built among cities that existed a few hundred years ago. We don't know much, but we know there were a *lot* more people back then. Imagine Arcadia but thousands of times bigger. There must have been millions of people, or at the very least, hundreds of thousands. Those buildings were built right next to each other, each one with hundreds of rooms."

Bast took advantage of her sister's brief pause to chime in. "Our grandfather said his grandfather helped demo some of them, and they pulled out the strangest furniture. Things were done a lot different back then. Many of the historical objects are housed in the capital today."

"As neat as all that is," Cleo said, a proud smile stretching across her face, "it's nothing compared to what lies beyond. Not even the new ancients dared to desecrate the sacred grounds by building on them."

Arryn's eyes widened, and Corrine seemed just as enthralled. She'd encouraged Dante to move faster so she could listen to the history lesson.

"What do you mean?" Corrine asked with the same wonder in her eyes that Arryn had in her own. "Sacred grounds?"

Cleo adjusted herself on her horse before continuing. "Our ancestors, as in our ancestors from *thousands* of years ago, built pyramids where the great pharaohs—or kings—of that time lived. My grandfather said magic didn't exist back then, so no one is sure how they were built. Each stone weighs more than a ton, but no human could have lifted them, even with help. It was a mystery then, and honestly, knowing what we know about how heavy stones are at that size, it's a mystery now.

"Our people didn't like the way the new ancients built their structures, though we appreciated the architecture. That's why we went back to building the way the old ancients did. There are several sites around Kemet we haven't touched. There is a city across the great river that was once the capital of Kemet, but for the most part, it hasn't been resettled. The center still holds all those tall buildings, though they are in ruins. The buildings along the outskirts of Jadid were smaller, so those were torn down and the usable resources taken for other things. The land in those places has healed and is now fertile again. Maybe we can take you there sometime. It's incredible to see all those giant buildings."

Arryn thought her head might explode. Arcadia was rich with history, but it only went back sixty-plus years. The Founder and three people he trusted had helped to create that city, but the history began there. No one knew a lot from before then.

Bast and Cleo had both known and had a relationship with their late grandfather, who in turn had known and had a relationship with his. That was well over a hundred years of history the twins had access to, just because they had a family who'd stayed in the area.

She thought of her father, and she wondered what he might have to teach her. He was a child when he'd come to Arcadia, so did he have any knowledge of where he'd come from? Had his parents shared any of their history with him that he could share with her? Corrine was in the same boat. Listening to the twins and the rich history Kemet had made her realize how little she'd used the greatest resource she had: the Chieftain.

Arryn continued to ride in silence as she listened to Bast and Cleo talk about their country. The more she heard, the more she silently prayed to the Matriarch she would be able to save it.

Three days had passed since Amara's parents were murdered in front of her eyes, and she hadn't come any closer to figuring out a plan to take revenge. Over and over, her mind replayed everything in gruesome detail. She hadn't been big enough or strong enough. There had been too many of them, and she couldn't help them. She'd failed.

She refused to fail again.

Revenge might not be a possibility in her current predicament, but planning an escape sure as hell was. She'd waited for three days, staying silent, keeping her eyes down, and pretending to be afraid. Doing so had made them trust her, trust that they had total control over her. In truth, the only thing she feared was dying before she got to kill that bastard who murdered her parents. Past that, she didn't care about much.

Several of the men, including Zuri, had left on a mission to trap one of those monsters, which gave her the perfect window. Part of her hoped Zuri failed and died in the process. In fact, for the greater good, she *wanted* that. She'd overheard the plans. She knew they wanted to bring it back and use it to kill others. Still, there was a desperate, greedy part of her that hoped he survived so she could be the one to do it. Looking into his eyes as the life faded from them was what she wanted most in the world.

A week ago, she'd been busy planting crops with her father, something she was incredible at and had a passion for. If someone had told her—Amara, the child who loved and respected everything about life—that in less than a week she'd be thinking horrible, murderous thoughts about someone she barely knew, she would have laughed and told them they were crazy.

But there she was, fighting to stay alive so she could get the revenge she so desperately wanted.

After several days of incredible acting, hardly anyone paid attention to Amara anymore. Everyone went on minding their own business. The men typically stuck to training, drinking, and leaving for a few hours to scout or recruit, while the few women in the group made food, served drinks, and entertained the men in other ways. It made her sick, but she'd been to some of the local small towns with her dad to sell. She knew what the world was like.

Sitting up in her tent, she dropped quietly to all fours and crawled to the door. She listened for several moments, waiting to see if anyone walked by. When no one did, she slowly poked her head out to see everyone was busy around the fire. Several men laughed as they told stories and held clearly uncomfortable women on their laps. Satisfied that everyone was preoccupied, she pulled back and tied the door to her tent shut, knowing no one would bother her for a while yet. They usually checked on her around midnight, when the moon was highest.

Amara quickly went to the back of her tent, pulling a makeshift bag she'd crafted from a sheet out from under her bedding. She'd stuffed extra rations of bread and fruit she'd stolen over the past twenty-four hours inside and hidden it. After tying her bag in a way that would allow her to carry it on her back, she turned toward the back wall of the tent.

She slowly stuck her hand into the sand in the corner and found the knife she'd stolen earlier that day and hidden parallel to the tent stake. After dusting it off, she quickly went to work cutting open the cloth in the corner, making two small horizontal cuts every eight or so inches. After a few moments, she was able to crawl out without being noticed.

To make sure no one caught on to her escape before midnight, Amara went to work tying the corner back together. The horizontal cuts had created a single strip on each side of the vertical cut, allowing her to hide the evidence of her escape. Unless someone inspected her tent closely, no one would notice, not even patrol if they walked around the back.

Once her tent was re-sealed, she listened for movement. The soft sound of shifting sand under large feet echoed on the opposite side of her tent. She ground her teeth as annoyance and anger radiated through her. She'd watched them for three days, and they'd been so predictable. Why was someone lurking around her tent now?

Leaning as close to her tent as she could, she quietly waited to see what would happen. *Please, whoever's listening, protect me.*

Memories of Amara's father dying while pleading for her life consumed her. She'd looked at him, begging him silently to let her help. It was possible he had been wrong. Maybe she *wasn't* too small or too weak. Maybe she could have saved him. But had her father been right, the men who took her would have known her secret.

She remembered her teary eyes staring into his, praying he'd nod at her. Praying he'd tell her it was okay, but he didn't. Instead, his eyes had locked onto hers, and he'd shaken his head. He didn't want her to give herself away. He'd done it to protect her, but deep down, she wondered if it was the wrong thing to do. She blamed herself for listening to him because things might have turned out differently for her parents if she'd disobeyed.

Sitting there, pressed against a poorly set up tent while

waiting for death to find her, Amara knew that if the worst happened, she would have no choice. She couldn't be discovered. She *had* to get away.

The footsteps grew closer, and her breath hitched in her chest. She could hear a belt adjusting as the objects he had strapped to it shifted and jingled. The man took almost two full steps past the back corner of her tent, looking into the sky as he prepared to piss. Her face scrunched as she imagined that smell lingering behind her tent while she slept had she not attempted escape.

One of the men by the fire howled in laughter, causing the man to stop fidgeting with his pants and look back. The moon was just high enough that he saw her hiding in the shadow of her tent out of the corner of his eye. He looked down and opened his mouth to speak, but Amara moved like a snake. Adrenaline exploded through her body with fear of being caught, forcing her to react without thinking.

Her eyes flashed from deep brown to light gray with green around the edges as her hands shot out in front of her. The man's eyes widened as he tried to take a deep breath to call out but was unable to do so. He clutched his chest as weakness took him. Within only a few moments, he fell to his knees. As he did, Amara was able to stare directly into his eyes.

"I know you," she whispered, recognizing him. He'd stood behind Zuri and laughed as he mentally tortured her father before killing him. "You helped him take everything from me."

The man gasped, trying to breathe, but Amara could feel him fading. Tears poured down her cheeks, and her innocence melted with every bit of the life she drained from the man before her.

"I imagine the desperation I feel pouring out of you is exactly what my father felt when he thought of you and your friends taking me away from him. You'll rot in hell with those demons from the south. May they drag your pathetic soul to the depths and torture you for eternity for what you've done to my family and others."

She took a deep breath and flexed her small body, and the rest of his life tore away from him as he collapsed to the ground. Since no one had come running, she imagined none of them had abilities like hers or any other type that allowed them to sense magic.

She quickly untied the corner of the tent and pulled the man inside before going out the back and tying it closed again. She was grateful her adrenaline hadn't yet settled since it gave an easy boost to her Kemetian physical magic, the school her father had known and taught to her.

Once she was finished, she listened for movement. This time, she heard nothing. Another surge of adrenaline pumped through her and her eyes flashed again. She allowed the magic to flow through her limbs as she propelled herself forward, running faster than she knew any of the others were capable of doing.

She wouldn't be able to keep it up for long, especially after draining someone's life, but if no one caught her, her magic would get her far enough away to be safe.

Then she would go to the capital to warn them. It had been the queen at their home that night. She'd tried to save Amara's family but had failed in the end. If Amara could aid the throne in finding Zuri and his men, maybe she would get the revenge she sought after all. That was all she could ask for.

CHAPTER FIFTEEN

Zuri and a large group of his most trusted men had spent two days traveling south. They told their plan to no one in the army. They were only told Zuri and the others were going to scout the portal and make sure nothing had come north.

Though several men volunteered to go with them, Zuri had made a big deal of it being his job to defend his people and that they should stay behind. It went a long way to make him seem even more admirable among the ranks.

As he and his men traveled, they watched carefully for any glowing red lights in the darkness. While it was far more dangerous to travel into the demons' territory at night, the portal was much easier to spot in darkness than in the daytime.

The hell portal glowed bright red and looked like a deep, bloody lightning bolt—an open gash in the world, floating just above the ground. Off in the distance, he saw the faint red glow, and his heart began to race. Behind him was his first in command, Asher, and behind him was a group of ten men, with an eleventh driving a horse-drawn cart with a large cage loaded in the bed.

Each man carried magitech rifles and magitech zappers they

would use if shit went south, but they hoped the tranquilizer they'd brought with them would be enough to take a red devil down. They had no idea what they would look for, but they hoped it was big enough to sound scary without posing much threat to them.

As they drew nearer, the faint glow got brighter, and Zuri signaled for his men to slow their pace. They had no idea where any of the demons were. It was possible they'd retreated inside the portal, but there was no way for them to know.

Zuri came to a stop and signaled for the others to do the same. At that point, they needed to go on foot, so they didn't risk the scent of the horses drawing any attention. He lifted his weapon as he stepped lightly. For all he knew, one of the bastards could be under the sand.

"*Pst*," Asher hissed from behind him.

Zuri turned, and Asher pointed toward the portal.

The leader's eyes widened as he saw the portal pulsing, the glow shifting and moving around it. A shadow moved inside, and he went on guard, the rest of his men following suit.

A long snout poked out of the portal. From what he could see in the moonlight, the creature was the color of blood. Its red irises gleamed in the moonlight as it stepped out, one large hoof after another. When it fully revealed itself, Zuri wondered what the hell it was.

The head reminded him of a rhino's; the shape was the same, aside from the razor-sharp tip to its snout. It curved down over the front of the mouth like the beak of a raptor and it looked armored, as did the rest of its head. It had two short, thick horns on its snout, much like a rhino's, and the body was similar, though the armoring was much thicker. He didn't have much to go on, but if he compared the horn sizes to that of a rhino, that beast was an adolescent.

His suspicions were confirmed as he watched another step through. This was three times as large, with long, bladed teeth that protruded over the bottom jaw. The horns on its snout were much larger, and the armor was thicker. He swallowed hard, wondering if he'd made a mistake. This was too much, even for him.

"I can't do this. I can't do this," one of his men said quietly behind him. His voice quivered, and Zuri could hear the fear in it. His subordinate was about to lose his shit and get them all killed in the process.

"Shut it," Asher scolded quietly. "Get your shit together, or we're all dead!"

Zuri turned to see the other man shake his head, his weapon lowering as he began to back away. "No. Uh-uh. I shouldn't have come. Oh, fuck. I can't do this. I can't do this."

"Shut the fuck up!" Zuri hissed.

"I'm outta here!" the man said before running as quickly as he could back toward the horses.

Zuri's head snapped forward to see the adult monster huff hard enough that the sand in front of him blew up in a cloud. It had spotted them.

"Shit," Zuri said a breath before the beast charged toward the running coward.

"Fuck! What now?" Asher asked, weapon raised.

Zuri nodded toward the big one. "We kill that one and take the little one."

"*Little* one?" Asher snorted. "That thing's fucking huge!"

"You wanna take the big one instead?" Zuri asked.

A scream ripped through the sky as the beast ran the other man through the back with its massive horn. It pierced his torso as the monster whipped its head straight up, flinging the man off the horn. The monster then caught him in its razor-sharp teeth before slinging him back and forth like a dog with prey. Blood and human shrapnel exploded in all directions as the body broke apart.

"How...the *fuck*...are we supposed to kill that thing?" Asher asked.

Zuri looked at the adolescent and saw the armored plates over its head and shoulders, extending across its back at an angle. For the most part, the abdomen was uncovered.

His heart began to pound in his chest as he thought of what he needed to do. When he turned back, the monster was moving to face them. It lowered its head like a bull, scraping a spiky hoof in the sand as it prepared to charge.

"Everyone split up. Kill the big one but save the little one if we can. Lay down cover fire. I need to get under that big bitch, so try not to shoot me. Got it?"

"What?" Asher asked, his eyes wide. "Look, I pride myself on being fearless, but that...that is straight-up stupid."

"It's either that or we get mulched into ground beef. Which is it?" Zuri glanced at Asher.

His second didn't have time to answer as the ground began to shake. The demon rushed forward, head down, to gore its next victim.

"Now!" Zuri shouted. Everyone raised their weapons and fired at the beast. The magitech shots hit the armor but did nothing besides make it angrier. "Jump out of the way before it gores you!"

Zuri dove out of the way, quickly scrambling to his feet. He had to find a way under that monster, but he couldn't see how. It was smart, he could tell that. If it were smart enough, it might know what its weaknesses were, so getting it to rear up or expose its underside in any other way would be nearly impossible.

He needed a decoy.

"Asher!" Zuri shouted. He watched the beast's every move as it charged past the line of men, who all tumbled out of the way. With its large size, it took some effort to slow its momentum to turn. "Asher! Get your ass over here. I need you to be a decoy."

His second in command looked at him incredulously. Even

with twenty feet between them in darkness, Zuri could see the expression.

"I'm serious. I need it to focus on you so I can get a good shot."

He looked over his shoulder to make sure the other one hadn't become a threat and that nothing else had come through the portal. They'd been lucky so far, but he didn't think that would last. The smell of blood was enough to draw any predator, and he didn't think these bastards would be any different. The baby didn't quite seem to know its size, and he was grateful for that.

Asher groaned loudly. "You get me dead, and I'm finding a way to return the favor."

"We have to get the underbelly. That's it's weakness," Zuri stated.

Without another word, Asher dropped to his knees, aiming and shooting his rifle at the monster's lower chest. It cried out and charged again. Zuri used the opportunity to run wide to hopefully stay out of its peripheral vision.

As Asher shot at it from the front, Zuri dropped and aimed. Only the front of the legs had the armored plates, so the backs were vulnerable. He smiled as he aimed just behind its shoulder. He fired, and the beast roared in pain as it tripped, rolling several times. Asher and the others once again had to dive out of the way.

It landed on its back momentarily, and Zuri jumped to his feet. Lifting his rifle, he fired three times into its abdomen as it struggled to roll back over. It cried out in pain again, the baby crying out along with it.

The moment Zuri heard the adolescent's screams, he smiled. It was horrifying. The parent sounded far worse, but the baby was terrifying all on its own. If they got it in the cage and away without any other interference, the plan would work perfectly.

Asher climbed to his feet and joined Zuri as they walked toward the beast, which was moaning weakly on the ground.

They both raised their magitech rifles and fired shot after shot until it finally went limp.

Movement out of the corner of his eye caught his attention, and he looked up, rifle pointed at the adolescent. It had started to charge but stopped immediately, seemingly understanding the situation. Zuri's eyes narrowed as he stared into its glowing red eyes.

"Go get a chunk of that coward Joseph and pour the sedative all over it," he demanded.

"Are you serious?" Asher asked. When Zuri nodded, Asher didn't bother to argue. He sighed and motioned to one of the men closest to him, ordering him to do it instead.

Zuri watched as the man brought Joseph's arm, struggling not to throw up as he did. "Good. Throw it to the baby."

The man did as he was told, and the baby jumped a little before cautiously sniffing it. After a few moments, the adolescent picked up the arm, watching Zuri and the others as it began to eat.

Two of his men vomited in the sand as they listened to the monster's jaws grind the bones as it chewed and swallowed. After a few minutes, the beast grew weaker. Zuri hoped the sedative would knock it out but wouldn't kill it. There was no way for him to know how it would react.

While none of his team had any real knowledge of magic, Asher's minuscule ability in physical magic was able to help them lift the unconscious beast into the wagon. The trip hadn't been perfect, but it had turned out much better than he'd imagined.

"Uh, boss?" one of his other men asked.

"What?" Zuri replied harshly, wiping the sweat from his forehead.

The man pointed toward the portal, and Zuri turned to see it pulsing again. He could see a much larger shadow as it moved forward, and cold chills raced through his body. He didn't think they'd get lucky twice.

"Go. Now. We need to get the fuck out of here," he ordered.

The man driving the wagon was the first to leave, the rest following on foot in a full run as they made their way toward their horses. Zuri hoped like hell that whatever was about to come through that gate held off for a few minutes. As he mounted his horse nearly a quarter-mile away, he saw something incredibly tall and broad move through the portal, rising to its full height once it was in the open.

"Fuck, fuck, fuck," he chanted as he kicked his horse hard.

He had no idea how big that demon was, but he thought it was twice as tall or more than the portal it had come through. Looking over his shoulder, he saw it pick something up and put it in its mouth. He wondered if it had just eaten the gigantic monster they'd killed not long before.

As he and his men fled, thanking Lady Luck the adolescent was sound asleep and wouldn't draw attention, Zuri hoped he hadn't just made an even bigger mistake. That he hadn't just led that and anything else that might come through the portal toward the north. Though the trip was a success, he couldn't help but wonder if he'd just shortened whatever timeline they had before.

CHAPTER SIXTEEN

In the last two days, Arryn had seen incredible structures. Large swaths of land were largely untouched, but along the river where the land was fertile, there were many small towns and smaller villages. They were usually met with kindness, though there were some who were leery of outsiders.

She was surprised Kemet had such beautiful fertile land. She'd expected a wasteland. They'd passed through some desert, and it was exactly as she'd expected. The twins informed her a large chunk of Kemet was covered in sand, but Arryn loved that most of their trip didn't require being stuck in that part of the country.

As they grew closer to the outskirts of what used to be a less populated area of the old capital, the larger structures Arryn saw in the distance grew bigger.

"What is that?" Corrine asked, pointing.

Bast smiled from her horse. "Those are pyramids. Kemet has many, but those are the largest. Remember when I said there was sacred land the new ancients dared not touch? There it is, the great pyramids of Giza. They were built thousands of years ago."

"As large as they are from here, I can only imagine how incredible they will be up close," Arryn said.

"You have no idea. There is an ancient area several days' ride south called the Valley of the Kings. Some of the greatest kings of ancient Kemet are buried there," Bast said. "When we get to Jadid, you'll see we have followed our ancestors' lead."

"The capital is not far from Giza," Cleo said. "We're almost there."

Arryn had noticed that Samuel seemed enamored of everything as much as she and Corrine were. While he was a cranky old rearick, he appreciated hard work and dedication. The Kemetians had that in spades, something his people had lost while seeking riches during Adrien's rule. They'd put all their time into the mines to make as much coin as they could, forgetting a bit of themselves in the process.

As the sun rose directly overhead, the group made their way to the great river to cool off and let the animals drink. Snow and Dante were both happy to take a swim, while Echo dove from overhead to catch herself a fish. Before the tigers exited the water, they managed to catch a nice snack, too.

Once they were finished, everyone applied olive oil to their skin to help protect them from the sun. While it wasn't perfect, it minimized the need for healing sunburn each evening.

Arryn thought back to her many travels. She'd been sequestered in the Frozen North, left for dead, and managed to find her way home. From all the way up there, she'd traveled to Kemet. From one extreme climate and landscape to the other, with thousands of miles between.

Over the last year, her life had changed more than she'd ever imagined, and that was never more evident than when they arrived at their destination and saw the thirty-foot-tall walls of Jadid. They stopped at a respectful distance while trying to regain their wits before going inside.

"Bitch and Bastard," Arryn whispered, looking at the tops of the walls.

The sun had nearly set by the time they arrived, but it still gave off enough light for her to see the soldiers posted every ten to twenty feet. She smiled when she saw bows on their backs, and she imagined they had swords on their hips. The guards at the gates were armed with staffs and strange semi-sickle-style swords on their hips.

"What the hell kinda weapon is 'at?" Samuel asked.

"It's called a *khopesh*," Amon answered. "I carry one of those as well. The curve along the inside is great for grabbing your enemies, while the outer curve is sharp enough to take off a head if needed."

Samuel's eyes lit up. "Well, I like it! I want one b'fore we leave this place."

Arryn and Cathillian both laughed, but Cathillian was the one who spoke. "All right, son. If you're *really* good, I'll get you one."

Arryn was embarrassed by how loud she snorted when she saw the look on Samuel's face as he slowly turned to stare Cathillian down.

"Lad, I swear to the Matriarch..." He shook his head, mumbling under his breath as he faced forward. Arryn was certain she heard him mutter something about Cat needing a ripe green switch applied to his behind.

Looking around, Arryn saw Bast and Cleo behind the wagon, whispering to one another. "Everything okay back there? We don't know our way around, so I was kinda depending on you two to lead the way." She smiled back, and both girls looked at her with concern on their faces.

"You might as well tell them," Amon called back, looking at the floor of the wagon with an amused smile on his face. "They were going to figure it out anyway."

Arryn's brows furrowed. "Tell us what?" She turned back to the twins. "Figure out what?"

Both twins sighed heavily, their eyes closing. Bast opened hers and looked at her sister before peeking around the wagon. "How did *you* know?"

Amon smiled again. "You're not as stealthy as you think. I had a feeling after hearing some whispers in my bar, but when you both acted stranger and stranger the closer to the city we got, my suspicions were confirmed."

"Ahem." Arryn exaggerated a throat-clear. "Again, I say, tell us what? Figure out what? Why were you being stealthy?"

The twins nudged their horses, urging them forward. They didn't dare look Arryn in the face, but each mumbled a quiet, "I'm sorry," as she passed. Though Arryn had many questions, she said nothing as they made their way forward.

Amon flicked the reins, urging his horses forward, and he looked down at Arryn. "C'mon. I have a feeling you won't want to miss this part."

With furrowed brows, Arryn sent a silent message for Snow to move forward. The group followed fifteen or so feet behind Bast and Cleo. Arryn badly wanted to peek into their minds and see what they'd hidden from her, but she respected their privacy. She just needed to be patient for a little longer.

Before they'd reached the wall, the guards at the gates shouted to those on top to open the gates and dropped to their knees, bowing their heads. Horns across the wall howled into the sky, alerting everyone inside to their arrival.

As the gates opened, Arryn saw a large group of armed guards on horses galloping toward the twins. As they brought their mounts to a halt, each guard bowed their head just as those at the gates had.

"What the hell?" Cathillian asked.

"Uh..." Arryn said, her jaw falling open as she watched the display. She had no idea what she was seeing.

Amon stopped the wagon at a respectful distance, and the rest of the animals followed suit. The guards looked behind the twins and eyed Arryn suspiciously, but Cleo pointed back as she spoke to them. The men's expressions immediately changed from concern to relief, or it seemed that way to Arryn.

After a few moments, the guards bowed again before moving back inside. Bast and Cleo looked back over their shoulders, Bast giving Arryn and Cat a guilty, toothy smile before turning back around.

The twins led the group through the gates and into Jadid. As their mounts walked along the road, Arryn watched in amazement as large groups of people gathered along the edge, everyone kneeling as they passed.

"What the hell is this?" she asked no one in particular. Her eyes flashed white as she connected to Bast. *You're royalty? Is that what this is?*

She saw Bast's head turn slightly as if debating turning around to look Arryn in the eye, but she didn't. Instead, she nodded. *Yes. We're the daughters of Queen Asim.*

Arryn's eyes widened. *You're freaking PRINCESSES?* Her mind spun. She never in a million years would have guessed the twins were princesses. She couldn't believe it.

"What is it?" Cathillian asked from Arryn's left.

"The twins..." she started, shaking her head in disbelief at what she was about to say. "They're princesses. They are the daughters of Queen Asim."

"What?" Corrine exclaimed. "*Princesses?*" She stared at the girls in awe.

Cathillian's eyes widened, then his expression turned thoughtful. "Well, if you think about it, it makes sense."

"Excuse me?" Arryn asked. "I remember the fairytales from Arcadia. Princesses do *not* act like Bast and Cleo."

Cathillian laughed. "Have you ever seen or known a princess in your life before them?"

Arryn shrugged. "I don't know. Does Talia count? She was a royal bitch. Pretty sure she thought of her father as a king, which would make her the princess in her little fantasy."

"Think about it. They came to us seeking help to save their land. Had they been peasants or farmers, it would have been to save their *own* land, not the country. They spoke about the late king and their patriarchal society and how things had started to change. They knew a *lot* about the land and history, including past kings. They're highly trained and very well educated. They had a presence that demanded respect, something that isn't rampant in commoners. There was a lot of mystery behind the twins, and this makes it all fit together."

There was a long pause as Arryn thought about what Cathillian had said. He wasn't wrong. The girls had presence, and they knew far too much about things that weren't what Arryn would consider typical about their homeland. Knowledge and training like they had were received in an expensive education.

"Fine. I see your point. Still, I don't understand why they'd hide it."

"Do you introduce yourself as a badass?" Corrine asked.

Arryn shot her a look. "Language. And no, but that's different."

Corrine shrugged. "Seems no different to me. If you go around introducing yourself by titles or what you can do to people, it might make them think differently of you. When you met me, did you see a sweet but lost druid child, or did you see a filthy dark druid who might be a danger to your people?"

Arryn swallowed hard, her words catching in her throat. Corrine was right. "I sensed goodness in you," Arryn said after several stunned moments. "But you're right, I did see a potential danger if you turned out to be a decoy or dangerous yourself."

"I meant you no harm. I went there to warn you and your people, but my dark druid heritage was evident in my skin, hair, and eyes. I couldn't hide it, even though I didn't want you to judge me on that. They were able to hide their titles, which didn't matter in the Dark Forest anyway." Corrine smiled.

"She's way too smart for an eight-year-old," Cathillian said.

Corrine shrugged. "I don't know how old I am. I could be older or younger. It's not like anyone taught me how to under-stand the passage of time before I left the Terres Forest, and my family never celebrated my day of birth. I just guessed based on my size."

Arryn smiled and reached out to squeeze the girl's hand. "That will change. I promise. You don't have to worry about anything like that again."

"Thank you," Corrine said. "Hmm..."

"What?" Arryn asked.

"Do you think I'm older?"

Cathillian laughed. "I wouldn't doubt it, with all that sass and wit, not to mention you're smarter than half the people I know. *Definitely* smarter than Sam."

"Hey! That's it, ye lil shite. Ye been a pesterin' me fer days."

Cathillian laughed again. "Well, you've been so quiet, I had to get you to talk somehow, didn't I?"

Samuel shook his head. "Yer lucky yer over there and that Arryn likes ye."

"I wouldn't go *that* far," Arryn said. "You can have him if you want him."

Cathillian's mouth dropped. "How dare you? I swear you give me away every chance you get. Keep at it, and I'll think you're serious."

"That's one hell of a way to make an impression on the people you came to save, arguing and ribbing each other to death back there," Cleo said.

That sobered Arryn as she looked around. She saw tears in many eyes, and some called out to the group, thanking them. The roar of voices had been so muddy that she hadn't been able to pick out what anyone was saying.

She mentally kicked herself for being so wrapped up in worrying about the twins' secret as well as joking with the guys. Her anxiety level was high, and she'd reverted to jokes and insults to cover it.

But now wasn't the time.

As they moved through the city, Arryn gasped as she got a

full, unobstructed view of a large pyramid. There was a large open area in the front and windows with balconies all over. While they'd modeled their pyramids after those of the old ancients, it was obvious they'd updated the design from the ones Arryn had seen.

To the north of the pyramid was a large shelter with at least ten long tables underneath, each one full of food. On the steps of the pyramid was a beautiful dark-skinned woman with perfect braids in an elegant up-do wearing long, billowy white robes.

Her hands went to her face, covering her mouth as she descended the stairs. Bast and Cleo climbed off their horses and ran to her, wrapping her in a tight hug.

"Welcome home!" the woman Arryn assumed was Queen Asim said. There was more than twenty feet between them and the others, but Arryn could still hear the love in the mother's voice.

The twins released their mother and turned toward Arryn and the others, waving them over. For the first time since Arryn had known them, she saw tears spill down their cheeks.

Snow and Dante lowered themselves to the ground, allowing Arryn and Corrine to climb down and make their way to the others. Cathillian, Samuel, and Amon all followed, Amon showing respect for their mission by allowing them to go first.

"You must be the help we so desperately need," the presumed queen said with a smile. She wiped away happy tears and stepped forward. "I'm Queen Asim. Welcome to our home."

Confused, Arryn stared awkwardly for a moment before bowing. The twins snorted as she straightened with a look of pure embarrassment on her face. "I'm Arryn. Nice to meet you. Sorry for the awkwardness. I was too busy *not knowing who you were.*" She eyed Bast and Cleo, and they both shrugged.

"You never asked," Cleo said.

Arryn looked at her incredulously. "Yes. That's how introductions are always done. 'Hi, I'm Arryn, are you a princess?'"

Asim glanced at her daughters. "You didn't tell them? I taught you better than to lie!" She looked at Arryn. "Please forgive my daughters for their rudeness."

"Did you... Did you just tell our mommy on us?" Bast asked.

Arryn crossed her arms over her chest. "I sure did, *Princess Bast.*"

Asim laughed, letting her head fall back a little. "I see you're a lot like my children." She took a step forward and placed an arm around Arryn to lead her toward the shelter house. "Come. There is much to discuss, and I fear there isn't a lot of time. I want to know all about you, your land, and your friends, and then we can talk about how we can stop the upcoming war."

CHAPTER SEVENTEEN

After checking the stables and making sure every house in their twenty-home community was safe, John made his way to his wife, Mariella. It was his turn to keep watch over everyone, but he needed to eat. When he walked through the front door, his wife smiled as she set a plate of hot food down on the table.

"Anything interesting tonight?" she asked.

He smiled. "Not unless you count a random sand cat getting into the stables and pestering the horses. I suppose that's a good thing, though. I'd much rather be bored than to have something exciting happen."

"That's certainly true," she said. "I just hate you being out there alone."

He shrugged as he crossed the room and gave her a quick kiss on the forehead when he reached her. "The odds of anything happening to us this far out is unlikely. We're a couple of days' travel away from where the monsters were reported, and we have all agreed to send messengers if that should change. We'll have plenty of time to evacuate. On top of that, with all the excitement going on south of us with the beasts, people are too afraid to wander around and rob people. There's no need to bother more than one person a night."

"What are we supposed to do if those things decide to come up this way? What if a messenger doesn't make it?" Mariella asked.

He sighed as a comforting smile crossed his face. "I know you're worried. You've been worried for weeks."

She nodded. "Well, before a few weeks ago, they only came out of there once every few weeks, and they weren't violent. They just sniffed around before going back in. In the last several weeks, there have been more than a few attacks, and they've killed everyone they ran into. They seem hellbent on destruction. Death." A chill ran through her.

John ran his fingers through her hair, gently cupping her face in his hands. "Would you feel better if we went to the capital?"

"The queen shut down the city. I've been able to buy and sell, but that's only outside the gates. I don't know if they're allowing anyone in anymore. I never checked."

"She sent notice to everyone that Jadid would close its borders but that anyone who wanted to seek shelter inside was welcome. I believe that stands. If you're that worried, we will go first thing tomorrow. Will that make you feel safer?" he asked, his eyes boring into hers.

She smiled softly and nodded. "It would. You're right, I don't think she would turn her back on us."

John was about to speak when a guttural growl ripped through the night. His eyes darted toward the door, and he looked back at his wife. "I think our timeline just moved up. Grab the bags, get on one of the horses, and go. *Now*."

Mariella's eyes were wide with panic as she gripped her husband's shirt, pulling him to her as he turned to run out the door. "Not without you! I won't go."

His eyes flashed blue as he placed a gentle hand on his wife's belly, which had the tiniest budding curve to it. "This isn't about us. You have to go. I'll be fine. I'll catch up soon."

Her brows furrowed as tears filled her eyes. She jumped as another loud roar rattled the windows. "I love you!" she said, kissing him. "You better not die."

He smiled. "Not a chance. I'll be right behind you. I have to warn the others."

Taking a deep breath as her husband ran out the door, Mariella hurried to their room and grabbed the emergency bag they had packed for this very reason. She slung it over her back and made her way out the back door of the house toward the stables.

She beat on every back door she came across until she saw magitech lights or lanterns come alive inside. That was the signal for people to get up and get the hell out. By the time she got to the last house, she saw a young man of about eighteen fleeing toward the stables.

As the final house in the community, someone inside was given the duty to grab a horse and ride as hard and as fast as they could to the next village and warn them to head toward Jadid and tell them hell had arrived on their doorsteps.

That should have happened for them, so the hellish beasts had either come through the desert and bypassed the communities, or far more likely, they'd killed everyone, and the messenger had failed to make it.

Within moments, she could hear people running out their doors as they scattered to do their duty before fleeing north. She'd done her part, now she had to protect her unborn child.

Without hesitation, Mariella ran into the stables and mounted her spotted mare, kicking her sides and riding as fast as she could toward Jadid. No more than a minute had passed before a much larger, much angrier roar tore through the night.

She looked back, her eyes widening as a shadow rose over the peak of the tallest house in their community.

John ran down the street, banging on the front door of every home on the western side of the road, knowing Mariella was doing the same at the back doors of those on the eastern side. He saw each house come alive, and families grabbed their things before rushing out and heading to the large stable that held nearly forty horses.

"Hey!" a man shouted from behind the eastern homes. "Hey! Is everyone up?"

John stopped the first man who ran by. "Beat on every door on this side. I'm going to see who that is and if they need help."

The man nodded before running down the street to continue John's job, though he saw most of them already being evacuated. Turning away, John ran between the houses and stopped at the corner, peeking in every direction to make sure he was safe before stepping past the shelter.

He saw a group of men standing forty or so feet away from the community, a large red lump of something lying on the ground. Deciding the risk might be worth it, he took a step forward. "Are you the ones who called out?"

A large medium-toned man with short, kinky hair stepped forward before hurriedly jogging the several feet between them. "Hi, I'm Zuri. Is everyone okay?"

John nodded, looking around him at the seemingly lifeless red lump on the ground. "We are. All the communities around here have a system set up if anything like this happens. We hear it, we don't ask questions. We run and warn the others. We have too many elderly people, women, and children who aren't able to fight." He pointed into the distance. "Is that the thing that made that noise?"

Zuri looked over his shoulder. "It is. We've been patrolling south of the capital. The queen shut down the city and isn't letting anyone in, so we took it upon ourselves to keep an eye on things. We happened to come into the area and saw that beast about to charge into your village."

"John," someone said behind him. He looked back to see a man cautiously watching Zuri. His focus turned back to John. "All the women, children, and elderly have been evacuated. What's going on?"

"It seems we have someone watching over us," John said.

Zuri held his hands up. "Unfortunately, I can't take too much credit. We found a body. I'm not sure if he was one of yours, but it's pretty bad. He was mangled terribly, and his insides... Well, I'm sure you don't want the details. We weren't in time to save him, but I'm happy we could save the rest."

"What about the evacuation?" the man behind them asked.

John turned. "Mariella and I had planned to leave in the morning. This evacuation needed to happen, even if it's just one of them. They found the community. We should all—"

John's words were cut off as a deafening roar forced all of them to cover their ears. He glanced at Zuri, who looked worried.

"There's another one?" John asked.

Zuri turned to his men, only to see one of them flee on horseback toward Jadid. He almost let loose a growl of his own at the cowardice, but he couldn't blame him. He wanted to run too, but he didn't think he'd get that option. Instead of worrying about the other man, he focused on keeping his calm, charismatic character in place. He needed the village man to trust him.

The intermittent clouds in the sky had partially covered the waning gibbous moon, hiding most of its light and casting long shadows in the darkness. Each man stepped farther away from the houses, looking toward the south to see an enormous shadow rise near the end of the row.

The clouds passed on, moving as if everything below were not about to become a bloodbath. As they did, the light illuminated a beast much larger than the one that lay dead on the ground.

It stood nearly twenty feet tall on what looked like a hybrid between human and dogs' legs. There was a slight curvature of the muscle at the top that moved into an overly curved knee that connected to an angled shin with clawed feet. Its upper body was long but humanoid, with broad shoulders rising into a thick, muscular neck. The head looked like it was part wolf, part man, with a shortened snout, elongated razorlike teeth, and horns extending from its forehead.

John's heart raced as he stared at it. It took a step toward their group, clenched its clawed fists tight, and tilted its head toward the sky as it loosed a hell-scream that shattered windows and forced the men to cover their ears once again.

He remembered his last moments with Mariella. His eyes had flashed blue as he called on his power while preparing to run out. He was ready for a fight if necessary, but the fight never came. Staring down the monster that had come to destroy their land, John's eyes once again flashed blue.

Turning to the men closest to the row of houses, he shouted, "Formation! *Now!*"

Zuri couldn't take his eyes off the monster, even as John shouted orders at his men. His worries had been justified. The beast had followed Zuri and his men north. While he'd thought it was possible after the beast came through the portal, he'd convinced himself they'd gotten away with it when it only ate what was dead without giving chase.

But he'd been wrong.

So very wrong.

The creature roared before taking a very large step forward as a dozen men ran between the houses to stand behind John. With no hesitation, John ordered his men to fan out. Scared as he was, Zuri wasn't about to let another man show him up, especially when the point of all this was to convince them to join him in his cause.

He shook off his shock and turned to his men. "Asher! You stay by me. Everyone else fan out!"

"Shouldn't we let them handle this? Looks like everyone here has magic, which we *don't* have," Asher said quietly to Zuri as he came to stand by his side.

"Fuck, no," Zuri said in a proud whisper. "I'm not about to let all this bullshit be for nothing. We had a plan, and we'll stick to it. Whatever they do, we have to do better. Look at them; they're warriors. We *need* them on our side. Now, get ready. You might not be good with your magic, but you're gonna have to use it."

Asher groaned as his eyes flashed black. "Great. Whatever you say."

"Aim!" Zuri shouted. "Find a weak spot, just like the other one!"

"Like the other one?" John asked, his eyes never leaving the large beast as it took another step forward. It looked as though it was sizing everyone up and trying to intimidate them at the same time.

It was an effective strategy.

"They're armored. The demon we killed earlier was an adolescent. We saw another just like it but three times the size. This, however, is a first. The other had a soft underbelly, so we need to find a way through its skin," Zuri said.

John nodded. "Good to know."

"I don't know what magic you and yours have, but if you keep it busy with that, we'll find that weakness."

"No problem," John responded.

"Fire!" Zuri shouted as he lifted his magitech rifle.

His men fired at the beast, earning a loud and painful roar from their target. The monster charged Zuri and his men, but John and the others intervened.

John squatted, his hands moving gracefully as the sand

responded to him. When he thrust his hands out, a large pocket of sand darted through the air, striking the monster in the face and temporarily blinding it.

Unable to see, the beast began to flail, sending three of John's men flying into a nearby house. The others shifted power through their legs and jumped higher than humanly possible without magic. While airborne, another of John's men was flung into the wide-open area west of them.

Zuri groaned as he took shots at every part of its body and failed to find a weak spot. He lowered his weapon, thinking about his next move. So far, the only thing he knew was vulnerable was the eyes. Shaking his head, he turned to Asher.

"I know what I have to do. Give me your khopesh," he ordered. Asher did as he was asked, handing him a sickle-shaped sword. "I need to get behind the bastard." He turned to John. "You guys have super-strength, right?"

John nodded.

"Good. Go for the knees while it can't see. Asher will pull him down, and I will get on its back."

"What do you plan to do?" John asked.

Zuri sighed. "Something really fucking stupid."

Just then, the beast charged Zuri. He briefly felt a hand on his arm when everything went black as a loud *crack* sounded. He blinked several times and realized he'd moved somewhere else without having flinched.

He looked at Asher. "Did you do that?"

Asher's eyes were wide. "I don't fucking have a clue how, but yes!"

Zuri smiled and turned to face the beast as he heard a guttural and pain-filled howl. John had once again sent a large ball of sand into the beast's eyes as his men attacked the legs. Heart racing, Zuri slung his rifle over his shoulder and unlashed his khopesh from his belt and stuck Asher's through it before running forward.

"Now, Asher!" he called.

He heard a loud grunt from behind him and saw the beast collapse to all fours. Zuri leapt onto its injured knee, then climbed onto its back. Praying to anyone who gave a damn about him at this point that the beast wouldn't overpower Asher's magic, Zuri ran toward its head.

Zuri straddled its neck just as it broke free of Asher's hold and drew the swords. "Fuck!" he shouted as he hooked the khopeshes around its horns and pulled himself onto the top of the beast's head. Before the monster could stand, he leaned forward and swung hard with both arms. The sharpened tips of the curved blades hooked in each large eye.

The beast screamed in pain, the noise overwhelming from his position. Another scream followed as it flailed, flinging Zuri off and shredding its eyes in its sockets in the process. Before Zuri landed, Asher was able to soften his landing with what little telekinesis he could summon.

Groaning, Zuri rolled over, leaving the gory swords in the sand as he grabbed his rifle from his back and took aim. The beast took several steps forward and then back, clawing at its face.

"Come on, you son of a bitch," Zuri snarled. "Lower your fucking hands."

The moment he spoke, the monster turned toward the sound and charged. Fueled by rage, it reached out in front of it, obviously hoping to get hold of Zuri. Its target, however, had other plans.

Zuri smiled as the monster's face was left wide open. He lifted his rifle, aimed at the damaged and vulnerable eyes, and pulled the trigger twice in rapid succession, watching in horror as the large beast lost its footing and began to fall.

"Asher!" he called as an invisible force pulled him out of the way.

Sand and earth exploded around the body as it hit the ground, everyone cheering as they celebrated taking it down. Zuri stood and lifted his rifle, carefully walking around to its head before shooting it several more times in each empty eye socket. He didn't want to take any chances.

"Tend to the wounded!" John called to his men, and they scattered. The local came to stand next to Zuri, inspecting the corpse. "That was a damn good plan. I'm glad you were here. We would never have survived that."

Zuri nodded, trying to calm his racing heart. He did his best to act stoic, but he was terrified. As long as no one else saw it, his plan was safe.

"You mentioned earlier the queen had shut her city and is refusing anyone," John said. "We just sent all of our loved ones there. What will happen to them?"

"You should send a messenger to stop them right away," Zuri said. "It won't be pretty if they try to get inside. I'm glad I came along because it seems you're in desperate need of an update, and we're in desperate need of people like you."

"Yeah? Why's that?" John demanded.

"Because if the queen has turned her back on us, and we're stuck between the Kemetian army and *those* things," he said, pointing at the dead hellbeast before them, "which fight do you think we have a better chance of winning?"

John took a deep breath and blew it out in a heavy sigh. "I suppose that's an accurate assessment. Go ahead. I'm listening."

Zuri fought a smile. Everything had gone to shit and they'd nearly died, but there it was—the opening he'd needed. With John's help, they'd have all the villages south of the city on their side. They'd have the numbers they needed to take down the queen and get his revenge for what they'd done to his son.

CHAPTER EIGHTEEN

Amara nearly cried when she saw the city walls in the distance. After leaving the enemy camp, she'd run on foot for several miles, healing herself when she needed rest so she could go farther. Eventually, she'd worn herself down far enough that using additional magic would be dangerous if she ran into another fight, so she made her way to the first village she could find along the river.

Going home wasn't an option. Going there to get supplies was dangerous because the men she'd run from would check there first, assuming she was a stupid kid. Instead, she snuck into a barn and soothed a horse, willing it to come with her without making a sound.

While she hated taking something that didn't belong to her, especially a horse, her life depended on it, and stopping to ask for permission could be catastrophic.

After two days of riding, stopping only when it was necessary for both of them to get some rest, she'd finally reached her destination. She'd never seen anything so beautiful. Those walls meant freedom.

"What is going on?" she wondered out loud when she saw the

closed gates, with guards posted on the ground and above along the wall. The great city was a place full of markets and trading. She'd never heard of the gates closed.

Taking a deep breath, she willed her pilfered horse to slowly walk up to the walls. Both guards stepped forward, their bodies rigid and powerful.

"Good morning," the one on the left said. "What business do you have in Jadid?"

Without thinking about how it would sound, she said, "I need to speak to the queen right away!"

The guards glanced at one another before looking back at her. Once again, it was the man on the left who addressed her. "Why don't you go find your mommy and daddy? Go. Get out of here."

She stared into his eyes for several moments. "That's why I'm here! She and the Queen's Guard came to my house several days ago, trying to catch a man named Zuri. He wasn't there, but they killed a few of his men, and one of them was Zuri's son. He came back for revenge and killed my parents. So *no*, I can't go find my mommy and daddy. They're dead. I have to warn the queen about Zuri!"

The other guard laughed. "That's one of the better stories I've heard. You're not coming into the city to beg and steal. Go home."

Jadid was supposed to be safe—a sanctuary—and they wouldn't let her in. "I thought Jadid was supposed to be a safe place for anyone under the queen's rule? Why the hell am I not one of those people?"

"Look, kid. A war is coming. The queen is working hard to make sure everyone—even you when the time comes—will be safe. We have to be careful who we let in and out. You're a cute kid, but you have no business in the city. Nothing good, anyway. Your parents aren't around, so you're playing the orphan card. You're filthy, and you have no possessions on you aside from what's on your back, so you're not coming to buy or sell. That tells me you're here to steal."

"But the queen was at—"

"Your house?" The guard laughed. "The queen has been here, working on something important. She hasn't left the city in months for safety reasons. Go. Now. Before I arrest you."

She laughed sarcastically. "Would that get me into the city?"

His brows furrowed. "Go."

She stared at him for a moment, thinking of anything that might help the situation, but all she could think of were insults and childishness. Finally, showing restraint she had no idea she possessed until that moment, she nodded and turned her horse away.

She began to ride south, unsure of what her next step should be. She stopped a quarter-mile or so later to think. A smile spread across her lips as she saw a black bird flying overhead. Her eyes flashed gray with green around the edges of her irises. The bird circled around and came to land on her extended arm.

"Hi, friend," she said. "I need your help. Can you fly around the city walls and find a place with weak defenses? I need a place big enough to sneak in without getting caught."

The bird squawked before taking off again. She waited nearly thirty minutes before she heard her new friend call from overhead. Excitement and worry filled her as she thought about what she might have to do. What she *would* do if the opportunity were there.

"Thank you for helping me," she said as she climbed off the horse. "Wait for me by the river. If I'm not back by the time the sun is at its highest, run back home to your family."

The horse snorted in response, nodding as it scratched its hoof in the sand. After giving the horse one last scratch behind the ears, she followed the bird's lead toward the center of the wall.

She reached out with her senses, feeling for any life force within the area. While she wasn't great with her abilities because no one had taught her how to use them, she had figured out a few tricks aside from her favorites: talking to animals and growing things.

Amara walked up to the wall and placed her hands against it, then closed her eyes and focused, trying to remember the magic her father had tried to teach her. Though he hadn't been very good, her father worked hard to teach her anything he knew that might be beneficial, and she needed it now.

"Come on," she whispered to herself. "Remember. You can do this."

It took her a few minutes, but she finally connected with the elements inside the wall. The concrete within a circle that was large enough for her to crawl through turned to powder and fell to the ground. As it brushed her feet and she smelled the plume of dust, she smiled and opened her eyes.

That smile melted when she saw a large, solid-metal plate that was no less than three inches thick and ran from base to top, and she had to assume through the entirety of the wall. It was brilliant. Several feet of concrete on either side encasing thick steel plating that had been salvaged from the old buildings in the new-ancients' cities.

"Damn," she said. "Plan B."

After locating the bird again, she made sure the area was clear before pulling grapes from her bag and burying them in the dirt. Her eyes flashed again, and she grew the grapevines up the side of the wall and scurried up. She moved as quickly as she could to the other side of the wall, using the vines to lower her to the street.

She took a deep breath, hoping no one saw as she reached back to touch the vine, willing it to pull back down the opposite side to hide her tracks. Her feathered friend flew away, and she silently cursed it for abandoning her so soon. There was no choice but to make her way blindly through the streets.

She kept getting turned around, and she wasn't tall enough to see over the people wandering the streets.

"Excuse me!" she said to a random woman passing by. "Where can I find the queen?"

The woman looked at her as if she were disgusted and wandered away. Amara sighed heavily and continued, stopping every so often to ask for help or directions, but no one would speak to her. Some told her to go beg somewhere else, some told her to leave Jadid and that she didn't belong, but most simply ignored her.

A loud screech sounded overhead, and she looked up to see an enormous raptor. Her eyes flashed as she reached out to it. The bird screeched again as it acknowledged her call.

Can you point me toward the palace? I can't see it from here. I need to see the queen.

She was met with confusion from the bird, which shocked her. The large raptor had a higher level of thinking than other animals she'd connected with, and she didn't seem fazed by Amara's magic. It seemed natural to her.

My parents were killed by some very bad men. Those men are going to hurt a lot *of people if I don't warn the queen. Please help me.*

The raptor sent her images of where to go before flying in that very direction. Amara wasn't sure what she'd find when she saw the queen, but she hoped she'd get another chance to inspect that bird. There was something special about her; she could feel it. She was confident she would find the answers to questions she never knew she wanted to ask.

CHAPTER NINETEEN

After everyone had a large breakfast, Queen Asim decided it was time to take the newcomers on a tour of the city. Arryn was excited because Bast and Cleo had told her about the underground tunnels and how the entire city had banded together to make it happen. While it had hurt Asim to cut off everyone from the outside, it had been necessary to keep the tunnels and their paths a secret.

The truth was, the tunnels were a potential weakness for the city, and if the information leaked, it could be devastating. The plan had always been to build them in secret and have trusted individuals lead the people through them. If the monsters came, the city gates would be opened for anyone and everyone to flee inside until they couldn't remain open any longer, and the newcomers would be welcomed into the tunnels before the entrance was slammed shut.

Arryn understood and thought it was wise of the queen to take such precautions. After all, had any information gotten into the wrong hands, an army could easily flood into Jadid without needing to touch the walls or fight a single guard.

"I can't wait to see everything," Arryn said.

"Me neither!" Corrine chimed in. She smiled from ear to ear. "Can we go see the giant pyramids? Or the ancient cities?"

The queen laughed. "Once this is all over, I would be happy to go with you to see the Great Pyramids. I would love to tell you all about them. Perhaps we could even take a long journey south to the Valley of the Kings. Such history there. The *new* ancient cities? Those are a little more complicated."

"Why is it complicated?" Corrine asked.

"The cities created by the new ancients are in ruins. They're home to the remnant," the queen responded.

Arryn looked at the twins incredulously. "And you were just gonna march us in there?"

Bast smiled and shrugged. "I thought you'd know that." When Arryn's sarcastic expression grew, Bast added, "Oh, come *on*. Don't tell me you're afraid of a fight with the remnant. After all we've been through?"

Cleo laughed. "Yeah, I didn't think it would be an issue, especially if we stuck to the outskirts. They pretty much keep to the cores of the cities unless they go hunting."

Asim sighed and shook her head. "I see your adventures have humbled you, girls." She smirked before turning to Arryn. "When our people moved away from the ancient capital of Kemet, it was to flee the remnant. My great-great-grandfather worked to bring the people together and tear down the least populated areas, using what they could to rebuild. Over the years, the fights with the remnant lessened as we forced them farther and farther away by destroying the outer parts of their cities."

"I'd think that would be an act of war for them. How did your ancestors avoid that?" Cathillian asked. "The remnant are very territorial."

"It was incredibly difficult. A lot of people died or were turned. It wasn't until the end of the Age of Madness that we began to flourish. That's when we were able to grow, and then came our magic, which made everything easier still."

Arryn was about to ask more about their magic when a loud screech echoed through the sky. Everyone looked up to see Cathillian's familiar fly overhead. She called again, and Cathillian's eyes flashed green.

"She says someone is looking for the queen," he reported.

"Who is it?" Asim asked as several Queen's Guard stepped forward alert and ready.

"It's...it's a teenage girl. Thirteen or fourteen at most," he said before turning to Arryn.

"A teenage girl?" Arryn repeated. "What does she want?"

There was a pause as Cathillian focused in again. "She said her parents were murdered by a man named Zuri, and she needs to warn the queen."

"Oh, no," Asim said.

"What is it?" Bast asked her mother.

"I went south to look into an issue we'd been made aware of. It turns out there was a man named Zuri recruiting an army. Some of his men showed, and there was a fight. A few of Zuri's men died, including his only son."

She bit at her bottom lip as her eyes closed for a moment. "If I had to guess, I'd say the little girl searching for me is the daughter of the couple whose house we fought at. We buried the dead and rushed back here with the prisoners. I sent a handful of men out to check on and guard them, but it was too late. Her parents had been killed, and she was nowhere to be found. I should have taken more men, enough I could have left some behind. This is my fault."

Asim's eyes became wet with tears she struggled to hold back. Rage filled her expression, but she seemed determined.

"There's something else," Cathillian said. Everyone turned eyes on him, but his focus was on Arryn. "She's a nature-magic user. It's weak, but she has it. Still, I could feel the remaining bit of the connection she created with Echo, and there's something off about it. I just don't know what."

Arryn nodded. "Well, I'd say we should figure out who she is and why her magic is off. Hopefully, it's nothing, but we can't be too sure with everything going on."

Asim nodded. "I agree."

"I can be of service in that department," Amon said. "If the girl will allow me, I will make sure she means no harm."

The queen nodded once before turning to one of her guards. "Shai, please follow Echo to the girl. Bring her to me but be subtle. There's no need to alert the people to anything just yet."

"And be gentle," Cathillian said. "From what I could see in Echo's thoughts, the girl is scared. Introduce yourself, and I have no doubt she'll go with you without issue."

It took twenty minutes or so for the guard to make his way through the city, locate the girl, and return. When they arrived, she seemed to be in much better spirits than Echo had reported. There was a smile on her face and a fresh apple with a few bites taken out of it in her hand. When she approached the queen, her expression turned serious and she knelt, lowering her eyes to the ground.

"Please rise, child," Asim said with a gentle smile, her voice soft and motherly. "Are you hungry? I see you have an apple, but you must be very hungry after traveling so far."

The girl's eyes lit up, and she nodded. As Asim guided the young girl toward the tables under the shelter, Arryn allowed her instincts to run. The girl seemed innocent. There didn't seem to be anything *bad* about her, but she noticed what Cathillian and Echo had. There was *something*.

"You're right," Arryn whispered to Cathillian as they walked behind the queen and the young girl. "I can't put my finger on it, but there's something there."

"I can," Corrine said flatly.

Arryn and Cathillian turned to their adopted daughter. Corrine's face was sad, her brows furrowed as she stared at the girl who appeared to be not much older than she was.

"What is it?" Arryn asked.

Corrine's neon-green irises faded to their normal green. "It's death."

Arryn's eyes widened briefly, unable to hide her surprise. "What do you mean?"

"When you were captured and I thought you were going to die, my fear and desperation allowed my healing energy to explode out of me," Corrine started.

"Mmhmm," Arryn responded with a nod. "You have an affinity for healing. You're the best healer we have, even among the Elders."

Corrine nodded. "That gift also allows me to see good and bad in people, just like you do. As you said, my affinity is healing. Mine is *life*." She pointed to the girl. "Hers is death."

A cold chill ran down Arryn's spine as she turned to look at the other young woman before turning back to Corrine. "Are you saying she's dangerous? Will she try to harm anyone?"

Corrine shook her head. "No, I don't think so. No one *good*, anyway. It's just what she's good at. She's like Jerick was. He *also* had an affinity for death, even though his powers were capable of growing and healing. The difference is he had a dark soul. He craved power. She seems to have a pure heart, and it's full of love. Unfortunately, her strongest ability is the death touch. I say that lightly because if I'm right, she doesn't even have to touch someone to kill them."

Cathillian and Arryn gasped. They were shocked. They had no idea the death touch could be so strong in someone who was inherently good.

Arryn turned to Amon, who stood behind them. "I have the ability, but I trust yours more than my own. Can you take a look?"

"I'll ask the girl. If she has nothing to hide, she'll grant me access. If she does not, I'd imagine the queen will order it. In either case, yes, though I prefer to do it with permission, especially with a child who has suffered trauma."

Arryn nodded. "Thank you. I appreciate that."

She admired Amon and his moral code. He was an honorable man, and with all the bad she'd seen in the world over the past year, she was grateful to meet someone like him. She was happy he'd accompanied them to the capital city.

They'd barely made it to Kemet, and everything seemed ready to head to hell in a handbasket. She couldn't help but think about what could have happened if they hadn't arrived when they did. More than that, she hoped and prayed she and the others would be able to make a difference.

CHAPTER TWENTY

After Asim finished speaking to Amara, Amon asked if she would allow him to look inside her mind and if it was okay if he showed Arryn how to as well. He explained his magic to her calmly, and his voice soothed even Arryn.

The girl granted them access without hesitation, though it seemed to Arryn it was more out of curiosity than wanting someone to dig around in her thoughts. As he looked through her memories, asking her questions to trigger certain images, Arryn watched and learned how to do the same. While she was uncertain she could do it on her own, at least not yet, she learned the process.

Concern had crossed Amon's face when he watched what had happened to Amara's family. Tears filled Arryn's cloudy eyes as she saw the images play out in her own mind. Watching the girl dragged away from her family, unsure of what might happen to her, broke Arryn's heart.

She had hope for the girl when she saw how fierce she'd been in the face of her captor, smarting off to Zuri and speaking her mind. The many trials she'd faced over the last few days was terrifying, but it was her final moments in the camp that broke both Arryn's and Amon's hearts.

They watched as young Amara was forced to defend herself, forced to use the dark magic she had access to despite being such a pure soul. Corrine had been right about everything. The girl *was* good, but she had an affinity for the death touch. It had barely weakened her.

Arryn shuddered as she thought of Amara's escape failing and Zuri learning of her dark power. He could have used her as a weapon. He could have nurtured that darkness, growing it inside the girl until she was as dark as Jerick and his brother Alaric.

Once things were settled with Amara, Queen Asim went to work creating battle plans. Amara had told the queen that Zuri planned to go south and get a monster. She'd overheard him discuss it with someone, but she didn't know what he planned to do with it.

If Zuri found a way to lure one up north, there was no telling what else he was capable of, and Asim refused to take any more chances with him. Subtlety wouldn't work. She needed to hunt him down and reclaim the loyalty of the people he'd so severely damaged.

Around nightfall, when the shift change was upon them, Arryn and her group helped Asim, and the twins set the tables under the shelter. She adored how loving the queen was to her people, and she took care of them with her own hands. She didn't order others to do it for her. Arryn admired that.

Just as they were about to settle in for dinner, a voice rose from the street. "Your Highness!"

Everyone turned to see three guards with a man in chains. Asim smiled at Amara and poured her a glass of water before making her way over.

"What is it? Who is this?" she asked.

"This is another of Zuri's men. He has a lot to say, both about

Zuri and about the portal and monsters," one of the guards told her.

Asim looked at Amon. "Would you accompany me to question this man? I believe you will get the truth, no matter what his traitorous mouth says. Normally, I wouldn't jump to such desperate measures right away, but given what the girl says and now this man, I fear time is not a luxury we have."

Amon bowed. "It would be an honor, Your Highness."

"Arryn, I know you're learning how to use your mental abilities, so you're more than welcome to join us," Asim said. She turned to the guards. "Take him to the jail. We'll be down soon."

The guards took the man toward the palace, and Arryn turned to the queen. "Your Highness, I would love to help, but I need to check in with Margit, a master mystic back at the temple. She knows more about those monsters than I do, and if that man has information, perhaps talking to her will help."

The queen nodded. "Whatever you need to do. I'm interested to see how their stories line up. I'm betting he'll be able to fill in the holes from Amara's story she wasn't aware of."

The city jail wasn't much different than the one in Arcadia, though it was about five times the size. With a city as large as Jadid, that was to be expected. Looking around made her think back to her brief period in the jail. She'd met Elon, and he'd helped her. He'd been the catalyst for every bad thing that had happened to her before going to the Dark Forest, but he'd helped her in the end.

While looking back on that time still angered her, she no longer held Elon responsible. He'd redeemed himself in more ways than one, even earning a pardon from Amelia. Arryn couldn't help but hope he'd found his son Gregory. She hoped he was able to repair the damage that had been done, but there was no way for her to know. She doubted she ever would.

When the prisoner was given permission to speak, it was like flood gates opened. She couldn't believe how chatty he was, and he didn't bother to hold back anything. Her eyes flashed white and Amon's flashed gray as they both searched the man's thoughts for any sign of lying, but Arryn could already tell that would be unnecessary.

"I know all this sounds crazy, but it's true!" he exclaimed. "Zuri has lost his shit!"

"What made you turn tail and come to Jadid?" the queen asked.

"He damn near got us all killed!" he said. "I repeat, he's lost his shit. The man is so grief-stricken over the loss of his son that he'll do anything to get revenge, even trapping one of those monsters and using it as bait. Everything was calm and calculated before, but his plans are extreme now. I'm pretty sure he's going to get everyone killed, with or without a fight with the crown."

The queen waved her hands. "Okay, just hold on. Start from the beginning."

The man took a deep breath, steeling himself. He slowly exhaled and began. "After Zuri figured out his son was dead, he demanded we go with him to the last place he was seen alive, just a group of his most trusted. He knew it would get bad, and he didn't want any of the outsiders to see him do his worst. When we got there, we found a family of three. Long story short, he killed the parents and took the girl. It wasn't until later that night that he figured out royal soldiers had been involved. The girl told us."

Asim nodded. "Yes. She said she told him that, though she purposely hid my being there. How was he able to bring a random girl back without raising any red flags?"

"Right. Well, we didn't know you were there. I didn't until this minute. As for the girl, Zuri passed her off to Asher, his right-hand man. Asher was instructed to keep her safe and away from the outsiders at all costs. She stayed in *our* camp in her own tent. Zuri told them her family abandoned her, and he planned to keep her until he found a safe place to take her. Those people were so shoved up his ass by then that they believed it."

He shifted in his seat, and Arryn listened to his racing thoughts. So far, everything had been accurate.

"Anyway, next thing I know, Zuri is *obsessed* with growing his numbers. He's been lying to people to trick them into joining for weeks, but it wasn't until recently that he became this crazy about it. He always did the same thing. He either showed up and played the good guy and convinced people the monsters were coming and they needed protection, or he'd create a scenario where he was the hero and come in to save the day and win them over that way. For an asshole, he's damn convincing at being the good guy."

"How large is the army?" Asim asked.

The man shrugged. "Depends on who you ask. He doesn't let anyone know anything unless it's his right-hand man, Asher. He lies to everyone else. I didn't know that until I asked someone one day and they said we had a few hundred. That was different than what Zuri had told me, so I asked someone else, and he said Zuri had told them nearly a thousand. So, I can't tell you. I swear it!"

Asim looked at Amon and Arryn and both nodded, confirming his words.

The man continued to explain everything that had happened since the death of Amara's parents. The trip to the portal, which from what Arryn had seen in her mind *was* quite far away, at least four or five days' on horseback from the great city. The terrifying part was the images she saw once they were at the portal.

The monster that came out was horrifying. It looked like a rhinoceros, but its back had larger plating and was hunched like a buffalo's. The larger of the two had long, razor-sharp teeth. It was terrifying, but she was happy they had found its weakness. If she ran into one In the future, she would know what to do.

Her magic was a hell of a lot better than that Asher guy's, so she was certain her team would fare much better. Though if her *last* battle was any indication, she might not be strong enough yet.

When he began to tell the queen about the botched plan to trick a small village into siding with them, she got chills down her spine. The deceit and brutal murder of an innocent man were bad enough, but when she saw what had followed them up north, it was all she could do to keep her heart from exploding from her chest.

Once again, Arryn began to worry about her abilities. She hadn't been in a fight since they'd arrived on the beach. Nearly a week had passed, and she'd used only minimal magic. In fact, the mental magic she'd used that day was the most she'd used the entire time. She'd never gone that long without training or a fight.

Anxiety crept through her as she wondered if she would be enough. She didn't worry much about Zuri, but she did worry about the monsters. If one had followed Zuri's group, it stood to reason there would be another. Maybe more.

"Excuse me," Arryn said, her eyes fading to their usual brown. "I need to speak to Margit right away."

The queen nodded once, and Arryn left the room. She went upstairs and leaned over, her hands resting on her knees as she closed her eyes and took several deep breaths.

"Ye doin' okay, kid?" Samuel asked.

She jumped. She hadn't realized he was there. He sat in a chair next to a vacant desk. He was the only one in the room.

"What are you doing here?" she asked.

He shrugged. "I figgered ye could use the support. Just had a feelin'. That blonde-haired beauty o' yers is out there teachin' the newest young lass about 'er magic. Bast and Cleo 'r helpin' with battle plans. I didn't wanna leave ye all alone in here."

She smiled. "Thank you."

Arryn walked over and flopped down on the floor next to Samuel. To both her surprise and his, she laid her head in his lap. At that moment, she needed comfort. It had been a long time since she'd felt so insecure, and she didn't understand why it had to come up now.

"I don't know what's wrong with me," she said.

"What do ye mean?"

"I haven't been right since we landed here. I walked into that fight on the beach... Well, I guess I should say I stumbled into it. I ran my mouth, made a big show of it, and damn near got my ass handed to me."

Samuel ran his hand through her hair. He was surprisingly gentle for such a gruff and grumpy rearick. "Ye've been in worse situations, yeah? You were left fer dead on a feckin' mountain, for Bitch's sake. What makes this fight so different?"

She thought his words over. "I don't know. I truly don't. From the bottom of my heart, I believe that if Corrine hadn't been there that day, I'd have died. Her healing saved me."

Samuel sighed. "Lass, I think yer in a new place with a whole different way o' life. Yer not yerself. Not ta mention, ye have a daughter now. Ye adopted her just as much as she adopted ye. That changes a person. Makes ye think twice before ye act."

She snorted. "Sure as shit didn't make me think twice before jumping into that fight on the beach. I was cocky. Sure of myself. There could have been twenty more of them, and I'd have acted the same way."

"Sounds like ye were humbled a bit. Yer not invincible, kid. Ye can die just like the rest of us."

She nodded. "That's what I'm terrified of. Holy shit, can you imagine me dying and leaving Corrine to be raised by *Cathillian*?"

A deep belly laugh filled the room as Samuel continued

stroking her hair. "Ye know I'd kidnap 'er before that happened. I'd tell his ma, though, cuz I ain't battlin' 'at one. No, ma'am."

Arryn smiled, wrapping her arms around the rearick's calf as she settled a bit more into the comfort he offered. She remembered doing the same with her father when she was a little girl and having a hard day. She wanted to laugh as she thought about the tiny things that equated to a bad day back then.

"I wouldn't want to take Elysia on either, but if you ran off with Corrine, I'm sure she'd understand." They both laughed. As it faded, another pause filled the room. "What if I can't shake this? What if this is me now? It's like a light turned off, you know?"

"I don't think this is it for you, lass. I think this is growth," he offered.

She snorted. "Growth? Fuck that. You can keep it. I don't want it if this is what it's like. What about you? You're older than me. Has anything like this ever happened to you?"

"When me daughter was alive, yes."

Arryn froze, her eyes closing as she mentally kicked herself. She'd forgotten he'd had a child. She'd died in a remnant attack. He blamed himself for not being there.

"I went on doin' things as normal. Everything was fine. I was the same badass I always was, or that's what I thought, anyway. I fought some remnant, but it was never much. One day, it was a lot, and I damn near died. If it wasn't for Sven, I surely would've."

"What happened after that?" she asked.

"When I almost died, all I saw flash before me eyes was me little lass. She'd be left without a daddy. Me fights weren't the same fer a while. I found meself holdin' back. Ye'd think it'd make ye fight harder, but I didn't. I took the safe route. I let others fight in front o' me. I did my part, but I sure as hell didn't run in first, and I sure as hell didn't take any risks. It took me a while to sort things out. Maybe that's yer problem. I'm no nosy mental-magic user, though, so take it fer whatever it's worth."

"I can't let this stop me. I can't. Bast and Cleo... They went all the way to the Dark Forest to find me. Then they waited for my return, helped us defeat the dark druids, helped us defend Arcadia, helped us defend the Heights, and then save the Daoine people. They've been patient and have been there for me at every turn. They sure as hell never backed down. All those fights were in new lands. Every. Last. One. Never did they let insecurities stop them. They deserve better."

Samuel placed a gentle hand under her chin and lifted it so she would look him in the eyes. "Then make sure they get it."

Such wisdom and concern shone in his eyes that it made her want to cry. She had her father back, but Samuel was a father figure to her, too. She was eternally grateful for him.

She nodded. "You're right." Sniffling, she unlocked her arms from around his leg and sat up. "I'm going to contact Margit. It's been over twenty-four hours, so I know she's likely to give me a mental thrashing." Arryn sighed, then gave Samuel a big smile. "Thank you."

He nodded. "Yer welcome, lass. Always. Talk to that ol' master o' yers. Maybe she can set yer head right."

Arryn laughed. "Let's hope."

CHAPTER TWENTY-ONE

Speaking to Margit hadn't gone as well as Arryn hoped. She came away with the information she'd wanted, but unfortunately, that information was scary as hell.

Arryn sent along the images she'd seen in the head of Zuri's man, and Margit recognized all of them. The four-legged beasts were overpowered, bloodthirsty, and built like tanks. Their underbelly was the best way to kill them, but it was nearly impossible to get a good shot. Margit recommended magic.

But Arryn couldn't use magic for everything. She'd learned that back on the beach.

Then there was the monstrous wolf-goat-man-thing that was over two stories tall, with a humanoid body and a smashed wolfish face with horns. Magitech fire bounced off it like it was nothing; its flesh seemed impenetrable. From what she'd seen, only the eyes were vulnerable.

Margit sent images of a similar monster she'd seen flashes of Hannah fighting in a place called New Romanov. They were everywhere, and Hannah and her crew fought them with no problem, though Margit hadn't seen how the battle ended. The mystic's knowledge of such things was limited, basically for purposes such as this one.

People sometimes compared Arryn to Hannah, but from what she'd heard, that wasn't the case. A smartass? Sure, they had that in common, but there was much more to it. Arcadia had taken from both of them, and they'd both worked their asses off to save those they cared about, but Hannah was a prodigy. She came from nothing, and she rose to be incredible.

Arryn still wondered sometimes if she knew what she was doing.

Taking a deep breath, she pushed her worried, insecure thoughts away and went to speak to the queen. Asim needed to know what Arryn had learned.

When she made her way outside, there were no less than a hundred guards standing in front of the palace steps as Asim gave them orders. They were her archers, and they were to line the southern wall and the southern corners of the eastern and western walls. She wanted as many as possible in the areas where there might be an attack. On all other sections of the walls, the archers were to stand no closer than thirty feet apart.

"Arryn," Asim said, turning to greet her with a forced but warm smile.

The druid made her way down the steps to stand next to the queen. "Forgive me for interrupting. I have information."

To the guards, Asim said, "Dismissed to stations," before turning back to Arryn. "It's no interruption. I welcome your input. From what Bast and Cleo have told me about you, I believe the Great Queen herself might have sent you. What did you learn?"

Arryn gave an awkward laugh and nodded. *Trust me, she would have sent someone else,* she thought.

"I spoke to Margit. It seems Julianne, as well as the Founder and his team, have seen some of the same monsters we have on their journeys. Margit only gets updates occasionally from the others, but they've shown her images that matched the ones I saw in the prisoner's mind."

"Did she have any information on how to kill them?" Asim asked.

Arryn shook her head. "Unfortunately, no. She said many of them have only a few places of weakness. A combination of magic and physical attacks seems to be the most effective way to bring them down, but if there are more than a couple..."

The queen sighed. "Fatigue."

Arryn nodded. "Yes. Battle magic is far different than training magic or what I'd imagine all of you use in the tunnels and such. From what the twins have told me, some of you use your magic all day during your shifts, and you're able to sustain it. I've seen them in battle, though. As strong as they are—and it's quite horrifying what they're capable of—they can't sustain it for long."

"Indeed. We use hard work as our training. Granted, most of our citizens have no idea how to use effective practical magic in a battle setting, but our soldiers and guards do. Bast and Cleo do, and so do I. We will do whatever it takes." She gave Arryn another warm smile. "I have faith that everything will turn out just fine. I have to."

Silence hung in the air for a moment as Arryn admired the queen. She was just a normal woman with a title. Family and duty were nearly equal to her, but Bast and Cleo were her everything. Even in a position of power, Asim was in the tunnels with her people every day until all hell started to break loose and she had to focus on her duties as a queen. She planned to go out and fight, as well. She wasn't the type to sit around and force someone else to die for her. Asim would never ask of anyone to do something she wasn't willing to do, and Arryn admired that.

Arryn prayed to the Matriarch she wouldn't let her down.

"If you were me, what would you do?" Asim asked. "Would you continue to reinforce the city and call all soldiers to action, waiting for your enemy to come to you? Or would you go out after them? Both have pros and cons."

"They do," Arryn agreed, nodding. She thought for a moment. "The object is to keep your people safe, yes?"

"Absolutely."

"Then I wouldn't wait. If you wait, you risk him being fully prepared for battle. You also risk him having more firepower. If he comes here, some of his men *will* make it through the wall, and some of your people will die. From some of the discussions I've overheard with you and those closest to you, the tunnels aren't ready yet. That means the people can't flee. People *will* die.

"Out there..." Arryn looked to the south at nothing in particular. "If we go to him, we're without the walls. We're more vulnerable, but we're more likely to catch him off-guard. If we get to him before he's fully prepared, we stand a better chance because we *still* don't have a clue what his army looks like." She sighed. "And there's something else."

"What is it?" Asim asked, obvious concern on her face.

"If we stay here, we could wait for another day or two, maybe even three or four. We have *no* idea when he will attack, which is a *huge* issue because of something else Margit said." She paused, reaching toward Asim. "Take my hands."

Asim hesitated only for a breath before taking Arryn's hands. The druid's eyes flashed white.

"I need to show you something if I can. I'm not the greatest at this yet, but I'm learning."

The queen nodded, and Arryn sent her a flood of images—the images she'd seen from Margit as well as the prisoner they'd interrogated earlier. Arryn heard an audible gasp, and she could feel the fear as it coursed through the queen.

"Zuri caught an adolescent monster by the portal and killed a larger one, more than likely the parent of the one he captured. When he did, something followed him up north and attacked that village. From what Margit said, those things normally only come once every few months as they test areas for threats. It becomes more frequent over time, but if more than one comes through..."

Arryn's eyes faded, and she pulled her hands back. The queen blinked a few times and shook her head, clearing her mind.

"If more than one comes through, it's a sign that war is coming. Given that *one* followed Zuri and the others up here..."

Asim's brows furrowed. "Another is sure to be close behind."

Arryn nodded. "At *least*. If we wait, we run the risk of fighting *both* wars at once. We can't afford that. We'd be overrun, and those beasts would come straight north. Kemet would be overrun." She cleared her throat, trying to regain her nerve. "So, if you're asking me what I think we should do, I believe we should leave as soon as possible. I think we should go after him."

Without hesitation, the queen squared her shoulders and nodded. "I agree. I'll get the soldiers ready, and you should prepare, too. You're going to lead them."

Arryn's eyes widened. "Me? What about the twins?"

Asim smiled. "They'll be right there with you, but you've seen far more war than I have. You've seen it more recently, too. You're the best choice. I trust you."

"Thank you, Your Highness," Arryn said, filled with both hope and worry. This would be an incredible opportunity to prove to herself she wasn't weak. It was also an opportunity to mess up if she wasn't careful.

Arryn felt a familiar presence overhead, and she reached out. She heard Echo's screech as she looped around and came to land on the rail next to her.

"Echo, can you fly south and look for Zuri's army? Get a good look at them so we can see their numbers. Then fly farther south to check out the portal. We need to know if there are any monsters coming up this way. *Please* make sure to stay high up, high enough you can disappear into the clouds if you have to. Don't get hurt. If you sense anything bad or you get worried, come back. Don't risk yourself, okay?"

Echo screeched and flew away. Arryn turned to Queen Asim. "There. That should give us some much-needed information. According to the prisoner, it's about two hundred and fifty miles south to the portal. She can fly pretty fast, so that'll give us about twelve hours round trip at a leisurely pace. Less if she books it."

The queen smiled. "See? Already making wise choices." She placed an arm around Arryn. "Now, let's get you fitted with some proper clothing, shall we?"

CHAPTER TWENTY-TWO

Arryn awoke to Cathillian gently brushing the hair out of her face so he could kiss her forehead. "Hey," he said softly. "Echo's back."

She groaned as she rolled over and snuggled into him. "Tell me she said everyone shook hands and agreed war was overrated, and they're going back to whatever hole they crawled out of."

His body jerked as he silently laughed. "I'm afraid not. I think we need to wake the queen for this one."

Another groan escaped her as she nodded. "Duty calls."

"Yep. Duty calls. Just think, we don't have anything promised to anyone after this. We can go on a nice vacation after we save Kemet, just the three of us. You, me, and Corrine. Mariana—the Storm Caller who sailed us to Kemet—told me about an ancient city where the water is so blue, it's the same color as her aquamarine eyes. We can relax on the beach and swim and play. Sound good?"

She smiled. "This is a first, you tempting me *out* of bed."

He laughed. "Yeah, well, there's a first time for everything."

"Fine," she said, placing a kiss on his bare chest. "You win."

"Oh, my. I didn't think I'd ever hear those words come out of your mouth," he said, moving to climb out of bed.

"Yeah, and I doubt you will again. After all, you're a child half the time, so enjoy it."

Arryn quickly climbed out of bed, grabbing clothes as she stumbled across the room in the near-darkness. The queen had given her a new casual wardrobe, made of the softest, most breathable material she'd ever worn. The fabric felt almost like wearing nothing. Weightless and airy, she didn't have to worry about heat. She had also been gifted proper attire for when they were ready to go to battle, but she planned to save that for later—no need to wear it just yet.

"So, what did Echo see?" she asked.

"I'll tell you when we get to the queen's chambers. I hate to wake her, but waiting would be a mistake in this case."

"*Oooh*, so mysterious." She joked because she was worried about what might happen. She needed to find time to meditate. For the first time since she'd initially been told about it, she felt it might be necessary and help her.

After lacing up her sandals, she pulled the robes down and stood, admiring herself in the moonlight. It was strange to wear something dresslike, but it was incredibly comfortable for Kemet with its hot climate.

They quickly left their room, knocking on doors as they made their way down the hall—Bast's, Cleo's, Samuel's, and then Amon's, though they avoided Corrine's and Amara's. Not that it mattered.

Amara opened her door, fully dressed. "Is it time? Is it happening?"

Arryn was shocked by the determination on the young girl's face. "No. Not time yet. We got news from Echo, and we're going to talk to the queen. You should go back to bed."

"With all due respect, no."

Arryn's brows lifted. She was taken aback by the fierceness behind the simple statement. "No?"

"No. I plan to see this to the end. That bastard killed my parents. I'm going to kill him." Amara took a step toward the door to emphasize her words.

Arryn inhaled, prepared to give her a speech, but she couldn't find the words. Instead, she said, "You understand how dangerous that will be, right? That you might not survive?"

"What do I have to live for? If I survive, I'll have all the time in the world to figure that out. If I die, then I died fighting for my family. You're here from half a world away. Something tells me you understand me better than you'd like to admit."

"She does," Corrine said from behind them. Arryn turned to see the young girl rub her eyes as she walked into the hall. "I love you, but you'd be a hypocrite if you told her no. She's thirteen and an orphan, just like you thought you were. How mad did you get when the Founder showed up in the Dark Forest and took Laurel instead of you? How mad were you when you weren't taken seriously?"

Arryn growled for a third time that morning. "That isn't fair, Corrine. You know that. I was young, and I didn't know any better. I *do* now."

"I don't mean to butt in," Cleo said. A smile spread across her face. "Never mind. Yes, I do. You train fighters from the time they're eight and let them get the shit kicked out of them when they're twelve by adults! This girl is old enough that she would have been in advanced training for over a year by now. I feel like the Arryn I met a few months ago would have said, 'Hell, yes!'"

Cleo wasn't wrong. Training in the Dark Forest was rough, but it wasn't war. Then again, when war came to them, young teenagers went into the trees to help defend the Forest while the younger children went with the elderly to be by the river.

Arryn nodded. "Fine." To the thirteen-year-old girl who was only a couple of inches shorter than she was, she said, "Where we come from, there are trials. If you can kick the ass of a fighter of *my* choosing, you can go."

"The *versuch*," Corrine told Amara. "You remember me telling you about that?"

Amara nodded. "Fine. Agreed. And if I win, I get to go? No tricks?"

Arryn shook her head. "No tricks. If there's one thing I'm good at, it's keeping promises."

With a single curt nod, Amara closed her door and fell in line behind Arryn, close to Corrine. Everyone was silent on the walk to the queen's room before Cathillian said something.

"Do you really think that's a good idea? The *versuch*? She won't be able to pass that. As far as we know, she has no fighting skills."

"Then she won't be able to go," Arryn replied.

"You know I love you, right?" Cathillian said. She eyed him suspiciously as she nodded. "Good, then you won't kill me when I tell you I think you're being overprotective. You've been different since we arrived in Kemet, and I think it's because you got worried you'd lose Corrine—or yourself, and then Corrine would lose you. You're pushing your emotions off on the girl."

"I'm trying to protect her, not suffocate her."

"I know she's thirteen, but where you come from and where I —" Arryn shot him a dirty look, and he held up his hands. "*We*. Where *we* come from, thirteen means something completely different. In Arcadia, everyone around you was busy buying the best and most expensive gown and pins to put all over it. They were worried about school and what boy they liked. In the Dark Forest, we trained for war. You know that."

"Here it's no different," Bast whispered as they strode down the halls. "We trained from a young age, even though our grandfather wasn't happy about it. Our mother wasn't either at first, but we won in the end. The boys begin to train young, and now the girls do, too. Kemet is full of remnant, so it's important everyone knows how to protect themselves. They also need to know how to build and sustain themselves.

"This is a matter of honor for her, not just 'my mommy and daddy are gone, and I want to punch the big bad man who did it.' Think of what she went through to escape. Think of *how* she escaped. She's *much* stronger than you're giving her credit for."

Arryn sighed. It had become abundantly clear that she was in the minority, and she understood why. She'd never allowed Corrine to run headfirst into battle, but over time, after she'd proven herself time and again, Arryn had loosened the reins. Corrine was incredibly strong, and she was a damn good fighter. Perhaps everyone was right, and she'd lost more of her edge than she thought.

Samuel's story came back to her, and she thought about how he was today. Fearless. Strong. That could have been because he no longer had a living child, but she didn't believe that. He had plenty to live for.

"Fine. The *versuch* will take place, but it'll be a test. I need to know where she stands in battle. I need to know if she can handle herself or if she needs to be next to one of us."

If that grumpy old fart can get his shit together, so can I.

Six hours wasn't long to sleep when war was coming and magic depended on rest above all else, but Arryn was grateful the queen managed to take it in stride. Waking her in the middle of the night wasn't their first choice, but since everything had become so time-sensitive, there was no other option.

"Well, good morning," she said, inviting everyone into her chambers. "Please leave the lights off. Find a place to sit. Forgive me for such unqueenlike behavior, but I'm going to lay my ass down because it's the middle of the night. Talk away."

Arryn looked around as everyone piled in, and she couldn't

help but stare. The four-poster bed had gauzy white material looped and strung all over the upper rails, and the bedding looked far more intricate than anything she'd seen in Arcadia. The room was full of stone furniture with red and gold silk pillows. On the shelves and tables were vases filled with beautiful, vibrant flowers, and some of the decorations looked ancient.

She badly wanted to inquire about the gold artifacts all over the room, but she kept her mouth shut. While she'd walked by the queen's chambers before with the twins, they hadn't shown her the room. It was everything she imagined royalty would have.

"Forgive the intrusion," Cathillian said, his voice stoic. Arryn found his serious battle-ready side just as attractive as his sense of humor. "Echo returned with news, and I don't believe it can wait until morning."

"Thank you for coming," the queen said. "If it weren't for this damned headache, I'd be far more energetic. I apologize if I seem cranky. Please continue."

Corrine's eyes glowed neon-green in the semi-darkness as her hand moved at her side. The queen gasped, and Arryn knew it was because of the heat flowing through her, even from across the room. Within seconds, Corrine's eyes faded to their normal color.

Asim cleared her throat. "Wow. So *that's* what that feels like." She sat up in bed. "You can turn on the lights now."

Samuel moved to turn on the magitech lights, and Cathillian continued, "From what I can tell from Echo's memories, Zuri's army is a hundred or more miles to the south. It looks like the report of a thousand or more men is closer to accurate than a few hundred. If I had to guess, that little trick he pulled down south with the captured beast earned him a lot of friends. Unfortunately, it came at a cost to the country.

"Farther south, by my estimation four or five days' ride from here, the beasts are getting braver. Echo covered several miles and spotted at least ten. We know nothing about those things other than they're bloodthirsty and destructive. Based on that alone, I hate to use the G-word again, but I'd guess when Zuri and his men killed the larger one right in front of the portal, the others smelled the blood and came through. It was an act of war."

"Makes sense ta me," Samuel said. "After all, if ye chum the water, the sharks'll come."

"How do you know anything about sharks, rearick?" Arryn asked with a smile.

He shrugged. "I learned a thing 'r two from the water dwellers on the beach."

She nodded. "I see. Well, he's not wrong. I'm not sure if they have a sense of loyalty to one another. It might not be that—an act of war, I mean. It might, however, just be that they've been searching for a fight, testing the area, but they found nothing. When Zuri attacked, they realized there's a fight on the other side. Or, they could just be testing the waters for something even bigger. We don't have a clue."

"I agree," Bast said. "We can sit around and guess all day, but it won't do us any good. We don't need to know why. We just need to know where and when. Our most immediate issue is Zuri."

"Hmm..." Arryn mumbled, shaking her head. "I hate to say it, but I think we have a bigger issue than that."

"What do you mean?" Asim asked.

"Everything we know says that Zuri's been lying to people and luring them into his ranks, right? Basically, you're the queen from hell. You abandoned your people and locked them out, and you're fine with sacrificing them to the big bad demons to the south while you sit in your cozy walled-in city. Does that sum it up?"

The queen nodded. "More or less. Not all of them are innocent. I've received reports of an increase in thefts down south. That was one more reason why I decided to close off the city. If one of those thieving bastards found out about our plans and possessed the same type of magic we use, they could sack the city in minutes without running into a single guard."

Arryn nodded. "Okay. So, *some* of the people in Zuri's army have been led astray, and we have *no* idea who is who. If we go out there with our magic and magitech blazing, we're bound to kill innocents. Farmers. Clothiers. Fishermen. Mothers. Fathers. People who believe their queen turned her back on them and have resorted to joining an army they normally wouldn't have to save their families from monsters Zuri has convinced them are coming to kill everyone."

Asim sighed as the weight of that knowledge settled on her shoulders. "This makes things much harder. A direct attack is impossible."

"We've run into this issue before," Cleo said. "In Arcadia."

"We did, but it was different. *All* of them were innocent. Scarlett had everyone under her spell. It was easy because we didn't have to pick and choose. We didn't have to play judge and jury to every single person we attacked. We went in *knowing* we had to use minimal force. Knock them out. This..." Arryn paused. "This will be *so* much harder. Some of those men are awful, like Zuri. Others are good."

"What about picking their images out of Zuri's guys' minds?" Amara asked. "You did that with me. Can you do that with them?"

"We can, but it will only give us a few," Amon said, his deep, calm voice washing over the room. "Zuri's men were captured or fled here before his army became what it is now. There are many they wouldn't know."

"Do you have messenger birds?" Cathillian asked.

The queen nodded. "We do. We have close to one hundred of them."

"Good," he said. "It might not help, but at least anyone who can be saved *will* be saved. Echo can carry a large bag with many letters, and she can fly much farther and much faster than any other bird. We'll send her farther south to drop off as many as she can to villages and single houses. Since she was down there today, she'll know where to drop them."

The queen looked more hopeful. "Yes! We can tell them it's too dangerous to stay south of Jadid and to seek refuge in the north. We can find more housing for them. If word spreads that I *haven't* put the city on hard lockdown, maybe some of those who Zuri turned will get out while they can."

Asim quickly wrote a letter on parchment before calling for Faraj. He came into the room, and she instructed him to have the soldiers work on them. They were all to say what was on that note.

As Faraj turned to leave, Cathillian stopped him. "Can you show me where the aviary is? I can tell the messenger birds where to fly based on what I've seen through Echo's eyes."

Faraj nodded and escorted Cathillian out of the room. The situation was fluid and ever-changing. It kept Arryn wondering what would happen next. Normally, she found that exciting, even though she took battle very seriously. With so much on the line and innocents at risk, she wanted to make sure they did everything they could to save anyone and everyone they could.

Her time was almost up.

She needed to reconnect to her magic and soon. Though she could use it, she'd become almost afraid of it. Afraid of being too weak and failing, and that could end up getting someone killed.

CHAPTER TWENTY-THREE

Z uri stood looking out at the unbelievable number of people in his camp. John's messenger had caught up to the women, children, and elderly who fled north toward the city. Instead, he had them go to a town roughly fifteen miles north of them. From there, word quickly spread of what happened, and more people joined the fight.

While a good portion of the people in his army had been loyal to the crown, quite a few had become skeptical since she'd locked down the city. No one knew what her plans were, and to keep them from the safety of the city walls was betrayal in their eyes.

Anyone who might have held out hope and believed the queen had good intentions was blinded by their fear of what had happened in John's small community. That fear overshadowed common sense, and that was more than enough for Zuri. He didn't give a damn if anyone other than his core group was loyal. He just needed their strength to get him into the city and to the queen.

One thing he knew about Asim—the one thing *everyone* knew about her—was that she wasn't the type to sit on the sidelines during battle. Zuri *knew* she'd be there, and he was glad about that. He wanted revenge for what her men did to his son. What she'd *ordered* them to do to his son. His death was on her hands, and since he had no idea who'd swung the sword, he'd have to do the next best thing.

Kill the bitch responsible for ordering it.

"What are we supposed to do?" Asher asked. "We have no experience commanding an army this damn big. We weren't planning for a turnout like this."

Zuri nodded. "Exactly. That means we have *options*." He stood, looking around at everyone sharpening weapons and inspecting armor. The women were busy patching anything that needed to be fixed, and the children were busy making sure everyone had drinks. "We need to figure out who here has magic and who doesn't. We need to separate magicians from archers from infantry."

"All right," Asher said, pursing his lips. "And then what? Once we get everyone sorted, do we head north? Because I gotta say, the longer we sit here, the more it feels like a huge risk. We have no idea if that was the only monster that came out of that portal."

"I know, but it's a risk either way. If we stay here, we risk the monsters finding us. The reason a lot of these people fled Jadid in the first place was that they believed living in smaller numbers meant less visibility. Now here we are with nearly two *thousand*. Those who were already established away from the city, like the farmers, were set, but everyone else has to be getting anxious, just like we are.

"Still, going north too soon could result in a catastrophe. We *need* to do this right. Think about what this could mean if we do."

"Trust me, I've thought a lot about it," Asher said. "Jadid would be ours."

Zuri nodded. "I know my mind has been scattered since losing my son. I focused on my revenge, and then on getting to safety and away from those red fucks down south, and then back to revenge, and then claiming a city. Regardless of how lost I am without him, my aim is true. That bitch *will* pay for what she's done, and I *will* sacrifice damn near anyone to see it happen. Are you with me?"

There was a brief pause before Asher nodded. "To the end. You know that."

"Good," Zuri said. "Let's start breaking everyone up and getting them into position. Once we have done that, we'll move north."

It took several hours, but Asher and a few others from Zuri's core group were able to fan out and break the men into sections. No matter what other talents an individual had, if he was a well-trained magician, he was placed with the magicians. Those with less control over their abilities were sectioned off by other strengths—fighting, archery, stealth.

Zuri's men were able to group seven hundred and fifty well-trained magicians in various schools, though eighty percent or more used Kemetian physical magic. Nearly two hundred and fifty were able to use a bow with moderate to excellent accuracy. The rest of the men were fighters with various levels of expertise. A few dozen were retired soldiers, and a few dozen more were scrappers from the streets of some of the larger towns up north. The rest were mediocre or relatively useful in hand-to-hand combat or with weapons.

Those men wouldn't stand a chance in one-on-one combat with a Kemetian soldier or Queen's Guard, but they'd do fine in groups. The queen's army was much stronger fighters, but he had her outnumbered nearly two to one.

He liked those odds.

"Everyone, listen up," Zuri said as he addressed his people. "I know many of you never imagined you'd be in a situation like this, where you have to fight for your right to live. Your *family's* right to live. But here we all are."

He paused, allowing his men who had dispersed through the crowd to reiterate what he'd said.

"We're caught between two enemies, the demons from the south and our queen to the north. She is the *one* person we are supposed to be able to depend on in times of crisis and danger, and she's failed us. All of us." He paused again, watching the expressions change on the men's faces. Some appeared sad, while others looked more determined.

"For months, we've feared the monsters to the south, and what help have we received? Some of you have said you received a *letter* telling you the city would close but you were always welcome." He laughed. "How did that go? How many of you have been turned away from the city? She has *betrayed* all of you! She protects only those within the castle walls, those who worship her without question!"

Mumbles of agreement erupted from the crowd, and Zuri heard several men support his claim.

"Those people are sheep. They follow her like lost puppies, like toddlers holding onto Mommy's skirts so they don't wander too far. *We* are *not* those people, which is why she closed us out! Who are we? Farmers. Armorers. Blacksmiths. People who are disposable until she needs us. She can replace us just like that," he said as he snapped his fingers.

"The queen and her men *hunted* me because she discovered I had enough intelligence to think for myself." Several men looked at one another before looking at Zuri again. Their expressions were inquisitive and concerned. "Over the last several weeks, I've gone from home to home, recruiting those I thought might help when the time came. I *never* expected that to happen so soon.

"Unfortunately, the queen somehow got wind of my growing popularity, and she couldn't have that." He paused again, watching them hold on to his every word. "She decided to hunt me down, and what did she find? My *son*. I sent my son on a mission to speak to a farmer about fifteen miles from here. When he arrived, the queen's men were there."

Zuri's throat tightened as he spoke. Though he'd wanted all the leverage he could get in his speech, this part wasn't faked. It was all too real, and he allowed the emotion to flow through him because he wanted them to see what she'd taken from him. More than anything, he wanted them to believe she might take it from them, too.

Still, embellishing wasn't a *bad* idea.

"Her men didn't give my son or our men the opportunity to speak. There was no chance for them to explain they were afraid of what was to the south. *No*. Her men just killed him. They killed all of them and *dumped their bodies* in the desert. They couldn't even be bothered to give them a proper funeral. My innocent son's body was not wrapped. He was not shown any respect, and they left him to rot in the Kemetian sun."

The men before him were overcome with anger. He could see it in their eyes. He wasn't about to let the heat in their hearts settle. There was fire there, and he needed to stoke it.

"When my son didn't return home to me, I took several of my men to the last place I knew he'd been. When I got there..." He cleared his throat. Some of his emotions were real, and he did his best to make them more dramatic. "When I got there, I was met by a seemingly nice couple. I spoke to them, and they lied straight to my face. Told me they knew nothing about my son. They'd never seen him."

He shook his head. "My men found blood all over their porch and along the side of their house. It was then that they said the queen's men had threatened their lives. That farm had a lot of resources, and she needed those. They had somehow followed our path and predicted we'd be there, and they killed my son to protect their resources and their precious queen, the woman who would see the rest of us die to save the rich people within her city."

"She'll pay for this!" a man shouted from the front, others cheering behind him.

"Yes, she will!" Zuri shouted back. "She's getting scared of the monsters to the south. I have *no* doubt she's heard of the most recent attack this far north. It won't take much time for her to come take the resources she needs. I'd imagine she's gathering her men right now, coming to take our lands!"

"She ain't takin' shit!" another man yelled as others yelled out similar sentiments.

"We need to strike *now* while we have a chance. If our queen is out to get us, to steal from us and let our parents and children *die*, what other choice do we have? We *must* take Jadid. We *must* save ourselves! Who's with me!"

Everyone screamed and shouted their support, and he was filled with excitement. Though he had no idea what would happen and what to expect, his plan had worked. There had been some bumps along the way, but he'd made it.

Now it was time to head north.

It was time to go to war.

CHAPTER TWENTY-FOUR

I t took nearly twenty-four hours to get everything fully ready. Everyone was armed with brand new weapons and equipped with brand new armor. Unlike in Arcadia, the clothing here was much lighter because of the heat. While Kemet didn't get as hot along the great river as it did farther out in the desert, the peak temperatures could reach over one hundred degrees Fahrenheit.

Because of this, they relied on wrist and shin bracers, shields, and their expertise. Like the druids, the Kemetian soldiers wore tight-fitting clothing with either no sleeves or short ones, and their pants did not cover their legs. Some ended just above the knee and some just below.

Twenty wagons were loaded with rations and barrels full of water for their journey. No soldier would carry more than his weapons and shield as they marched to the south.

The past twenty-four hours had been interesting for Arryn because Bast and Cleo had demanded she join in their pre-battle ritual. In the Dark Forest, Arryn had introduced them to many new things, and the tables had turned. It was their turn.

Arryn and Corrine joined the twins and their mother in the queen's chambers. When they arrived, they were all in comfortable, loose-fitting clothes, and the queen's hair was loose. Corrine and Cleo had both recently had their hair re-braided, but it had been quite a while since the queen had, and Arryn had never had hers done.

"This is how we spend time together before battle or before we do anything overly important. It helps us center ourselves and allows us to bond before we face hardship or threats," the queen had told her.

"We wear our hair like this because it's protective for our hair type, especially out in hot temperatures and around a lot of sand and dirt. Your hair is too straight to hold braids like ours properly, but there are other types we can do."

Cleo took to cleaning and brushing her mother's hair, putting special oils in it to keep it healthy and shiny. Bast went to work on Arryn. She first washed her hair and combed it, skipping the oils because it would have made her hair too slick to hold whatever style Bast chose for her. Then she sectioned off her hair and went to work.

It took hours for them to work through the queen's hair, but it was no different from Cleo's or Corrine's braids. Arryn was always grateful to take part in their braiding sessions by sitting with them and keeping them company, but she'd never been included in such a way before. She felt it was wrong to intrude, given that Corrine's heritage was so much different from her own.

Being invited to join them before a big battle meant more to Arryn than she could express.

Just before Arryn left the queen's chambers that night, Asim had stopped Arryn to speak with her alone.

"The girls told me about your plans for Amara."

Arryn nodded. "Yes. I think it's important. I'm worried about her safety, and I don't think she should be sent out on a battlefield at thirteen years old."

"Where you're from, you have many traditions. I have to say, learning about your homeland gave me a greater appreciation for you.

It's not too far from what we have here. Once this battle with Zuri is over, I'd like to show you." She paused. "We have a lot of traditions here, too."

"I hope this doesn't come off as rude but are you saying there's a tradition for sending a thirteen-year-old girl into battle with no experience?"

The queen shook her head. "No, there isn't. We have orphaned children all over Kemet. I'm sure you've met your fair share of orphans from the city of magic. Arcadia, was it?" Arryn nodded and Asim paused, then, *"The orphans here have no families, but we care for them as much as we can. There are carts of food and water just for them, and they're taught where they can go so they don't have to steal.*

"That girl is an orphan now. She has no one and nothing. She lost everything, and the only request she has is to avenge her fallen family. Like you, I'm not happy to send a thirteen-year-old girl into battle, but I'm confident she can take care of herself. She's capable of using powerful nature magic, and she can also use Kemetian magic. Not only that, but she knows how to use a knife and a bow."

Arryn thought about the queen's words, and she knew what was coming. "Are you saying you want her to join us?"

Asim nodded. "Yes. I've never been one to stomp my foot and make commands, but I believe this will hang over her head for a long time— maybe even forever—if she isn't allowed to go." The queen stared into Arryn's worried eyes. "Do you plan to bring Corrine?"

A tingle went down Arryn's spine as her body stiffened. She didn't want to think about that any more than she wanted to think about Amara going in. "No."

"Even though she's the most powerful healer we have and could save countless lives?"

"She's a child," Arryn said quietly. "Or so I keep telling myself." She sighed. "She's seen enough blood and death to last anyone a lifetime. Somehow, it doesn't seem to bother her."

Asim smiled. "That's because she's a warrior, just like her mother. You've taught her well in the short time she's been in your life."

"There won't be trees and plants out there to save her. She can't hide high in the branches when things get bad. This is very different from anything she's been part of."

"Being a mother means balancing what is necessary for your child and what they need for themselves. You're not a rich noble, worrying about which foods are best and what her attire will say about her personality or station in life. Those things don't matter to her. Being useful and being able to save lives and fight for what's right is what's most important to her. You will have to decide if the benefits outweigh the risks."

Arryn smiled. "I'm not sure she wouldn't sneak off in one of the wagons."

Asim laughed. "Mother to mother? Both Corrine and Amara have been caught in the wagons already. Twice."

A hand on Arryn's arm startled her out of her thoughts, and she looked over to see Corrine standing next to her. She had a small shield on her back, along with daggers on both hips. She looked like she was ready to take on the world.

"I'm ready," she said, confirming Arryn's thoughts.

Arryn nodded. "You know the risks, right? And Cathillian went over everything with you?"

Her daughter nodded. "Yes. I know what to do." She squeezed Arryn's arm. "I know this hurts you. I can see it in your face, but I'm ready. I know what happened at the beach scared you, but we weren't prepared. This time, we are. We've had nearly two weeks to rest since then, and neither of us has used much magic. I've trained with Bast and Cleo, but that's it. Nothing else."

"I'm not hurt, I'm terrified. I haven't used *any* magic for training aside from mental magic to connect to Margit, and also to look into Amara and that prisoner. I've been too scared to touch it or even train. I was scared I might not recover enough before a big fight happened if I didn't. Those are the things I'm afraid of for me. My fears about what could happen to you?" Arryn shook her head. "They don't compare."

Corrine gave a small smile. "I've fought Nika. I've fought you, Cathillian, and some of the best fighters my age and older back in the Forest. I've also trained with the twins. A *lot*. Believe it or not, I'm pretty good at learning magic. You haven't tested me in a long time, so you're not aware of what I can do now."

Though she knew the girl hadn't meant to, those words cut her. As her caretaker, she felt as though she should know everything about her child. She'd been so worried about everything else going on that she'd missed some of Corrine growing up and how she'd blossomed with her abilities.

"Trust me, Mom. When you see me out there, you won't doubt me—or yourself. We *can* do this. You're *Arryn*. You eat bad guys for breakfast. Don't let them take that confidence from you."

Arryn smiled and pulled Corrine into a hug. "I'm doing this for you since you and everyone else thinks you're ready. I don't doubt you, not even a little, but that doesn't mean I'm not scared as hell."

"And that's why nothin's gonna happen ta any of our lasses," Samuel said from behind them. Arryn turned, wiping stray tears from her cheeks. The rearick handed her the *Heilig* tree bow and quiver. "Suit up, lass. It's time ta get ta work."

Slinging the quiver over her shoulder and then her bow, she said, "You're damn right it is."

CHAPTER TWENTY-FIVE

This part was familiar to Arryn. She'd marched toward battle many times. It felt natural to her, and she welcomed it. Riding on Snow's back with her warrior daughter beside her on an even larger Dante somehow braced her. She didn't feel worried. That was gone, replaced by determination.

The fat moody rabbit sat behind Corrine on the enormous tiger's back, riding into battle with his human, but it was obvious the girl had yet to realize it. Cathillian told her it was rare for kids as young as her to bond with an animal, though many kids had a deep connection to a specific animal until they were older and a bond could form.

He'd said it was possible she might not feel it or understand it, but she would. The bond was different for everyone, and it presented in different ways. It had taken Arryn several days to connect to her tigers, maybe longer. She honestly couldn't remember, but she remembered worrying she might not wake up every time she fell asleep in that cave with them. It wasn't until she began accidentally seeing through their eyes that she'd realized what had happened.

Corrine had been in the process of bonding with Not-Rodney

for over a month. She and Cathillian could tell because of his increased size and the random changes in the colors of his fur. Corrine's magic had somehow changed him in a way that allowed him to subtly camouflage the bottom part of his legs and his paws.

Arryn planned to have a conversation with her daughter once this battle was over and there was time to calm down.

The army stopped just before daylight and rested for a few hours. They had no idea how much longer they would have to travel, and the soldiers needed food and sleep before the sun rose too high.

After about six hours, the heat began to climb inside the tents, and the camp was quickly broken down before getting back to traveling. While Arryn was grateful for the Zen time before battle, she was also miserable. She just wanted to get it all over with.

The answer to her silent prayers came a few short hours later when the first line halted, and everyone else responded the same way. As leader, Arryn rode to the front. Heat rose from the sand, making the air look wavy, but in the distance, she was able to make out a distinct line moving across the desert.

The queen rode up beside Arryn, and she turned. "Is that the horizon playing tricks on me, or is that a line of soldiers?" Arryn asked.

Asim nodded. "I don't think it's a trick. I believe that is the army we were warned about. It also looks as though the letters we sent out didn't reach the men."

Echo and many other messenger birds were sent out to deliver the word that anyone was welcome to come to Jadid for safety. Asim had warned them that war was about to break out, and she wanted to keep her people safe. Hundreds of people fled to the city, and like anyone else who sought shelter within its walls, they were given temporary housing until everything blew over.

"Either that or they didn't believe it. I couldn't imagine sending their families to a place they believed they were going to conquer," Arryn said.

"If I had to take a wild guess, I'd say those who showed up at the gates were north of Zuri's men. These poor souls believe they've been forgotten."

"My Queen," Faraj said to Asim's left. "They're running."

Asim looked Arryn in the eyes. "Are you ready for this?"

"Absolutely," she said, though she wanted to say something else. She was as ready as she could be. Regardless of her fears, she was ready to test herself again. It was time.

"Say something," Asim directed, gesturing.

Arryn nodded and silently urged Snow to turn so they could face the soldiers. "It's time to fight for Jadid. For *all* of Kemet," she called out. "Everyone stand ready. I want shields up and archers to move forward. Remember, some of those men are innocent, so let's see if we can intimidate them before killing them. Protect who we can, but don't risk yourselves. Let's go!"

Snow ran back through the men, and they closed the gap behind her, creating a shield wall as the archers stepped forward. Though she couldn't sense the vibrations in the earth like the Kemetians could, she did sense the enemy's collective life force rushing forward before they stopped.

"Hold!" Arryn called, confused as to why a large army ran so quickly, only to stop. Her eyes flashed white as she reached out to the man closest to her on the enemy side. It took only seconds to learn their plan. "They have archers!"

Two shadows covered the area as Bast and Cleo leapt in front of the shield wall. They landed hard in the sand but recovered quickly and moved in unison as they forced their fists into the sand before thrusting them into the sky. A massive wall of sand lifted and obscured each side's view of the other.

That won't stop the archers, Arryn sent quickly.

No, but it sure as hell throws them off. Now's our chance to get the upper hand, Cleo responded.

Arryn couldn't agree more. Without wasting much energy, she sent a mental order to several in the front line to charge forward as she signaled with both hands for anyone behind her to move.

Shields were lifted and the soldiers began to charge, their footsteps muffled by the sand. Without any hesitation, the Queen's Soldiers blew through the wall of sand to the other side just as Arryn heard the loud *thwap* of several hundred bows. The sky was dotted with arrows, but Cathillian was fast.

With a wave of his hand, a large gust of wind blew through, knocking all the arrows off course so they simply fell to the ground, limiting injuries to scrapes rather than piercing wounds. Arryn had expected a large amount of sand to move through with the wind, but the powerful Kemetian magicians had anticipated his movement and kept the sand on the ground.

"All right, Snow. Are you ready?" Arryn asked. The tiger growled loudly in response, and she nodded before turning to the archers. "Change of plans! No blind shots. Stay low and take out their archers—non-lethal shots if you can."

Looking back, she saw Corrine and Amara sitting on their mounts beside one another. Arryn's eyes flashed white again as she spoke to them. *Stay vigilant. Use your energy sparingly, and for the love of God, Corrine, don't heal anyone too much!*

Both girls nodded, and Arryn urged Snow to run toward the battle. Cathillian was quick to join her on Maia. As the horse ran, he stood on her back in a crouch, holding onto her mane.

When they got close to the fighting, the horse stopped and bucked hard, and Cathillian pushed off at the same time. He flipped over in the air once and unsheathed his sword before disappearing into the crowd.

"Let's not do that," Arryn said as she and Snow arrived. "But *do* let 'em know we're comin.'"

Snow loosed a loud growl that sounded like death. Several men turned in horror as they saw the large tiger charge through their line. Arryn slashed at people with her ram's-horn daggers as Snow took several out with her large paws as well as her powerful jaws.

"Non-lethal if you can manage it," Arryn warned Snow as they came to a clearing large enough for her to slide off the big cat's back.

Snow growled her acknowledgment before running into the crowd and taking down three more men in a single leap.

Arryn felt a presence behind her, and she dodged a swipe from one of those swords Amon had told her about, the khopesh. It looked horrifying as he swung it.

"Now or never," she said to herself as she ducked another swing.

Taking a deep breath, she dropped to her knees and used an old favorite—jabbing her attacker between the legs before twisting her body so her back faced him. As he predictably leaned over, still groaning, she reached up with both hands and wrapped her arms around his head before pulling him over her shoulders to land hard on his back.

"The queen is *not* your enemy! Zuri is!" she blurted.

"Bullshit!" he ground out as he grabbed her thin shirt, ripping the straps on her right shoulder as he pulled her down. He quickly scrambled onto his knees.

"I could have killed you," she continued as she rolled out of the way of his downward strike, slinging sand everywhere with her braids.

"Bullshit!" he said again. "The bitch tried to sacrifice us to the demons!"

Arryn cried out as she leapt at him from her position on her knees. His eyes widened as she landed hard on him, kneeing him again in the groin. "Zuri is using all of you to sack the city! If she wanted you dead, I'd have killed you!"

He laughed. "That's cute," he said before headbutting her in the face.

She cried out as she saw her blood spray out with what little vision remained and the battle on the beach came back to her. Anger washed through her, and she knew she had to channel it before she killed an innocent man.

Opening her senses, she felt several dark souls in her midst, and she smiled. The man on the ground reached for her, but her eyes flashed black, startling him for a moment before she vanished with a loud *crack!*

She reappeared in the opening a few feet away, her irises clouding over and bleeding into the black. She sent a quick non-verbal threat to the men she'd targeted as killers, and they quickly turned to find what had alerted their senses.

There were four of them, and she remembered the last time her odds seemed so easy. This time, she wouldn't underestimate them. She wouldn't make the same mistake twice.

One charged forward, and she ducked his swing before punching him hard in the side. She grabbed the spare sword he had on his hip and unsheathed it before slashing it across his neck and chest as he turned. As he dropped, she twisted both of her hands, a bright blue fireball appearing in each one. She threw one at one of the men who ran.

She then turned to face the man still on the ground, his eyes wide with confusion as she took the second fireball and dropped to her knees, forcing her fist in the sand. When she raised it, she pulled a long shard of glass free. The other two men she'd targeted shifted back and forth as they anticipated her movements, but she knew they couldn't anticipate this.

"You've turned innocent men into murderers, and for what? For Zuri? You've damned your own souls, but you didn't have to damn all the others."

The men laughed. "There are twice as many of us as there are of you, and this isn't even all of us. You can't save them all."

She smiled. "Oh, but I'm gonna try."

She lifted the glass spike into the air and clenched her free fist, shattering it into dozens of pieces that suspended in the air. Her opponents' expressions fell as she flicked her wrist, the shards cutting through them like butter before dropping them to the ground.

Once again, she turned to the man on the ground, her eyes fading to their normal color. She walked over and offered him a hand. "Like I said, if the queen wanted you dead, you would be. My goal is to save as many of you as I can. Zuri's men are fair game, though. I won't hesitate to take them out."

The man accepted her hand and stood. "What can I do?"

"Get to as many of your men as you can and do your best to stop them. Believe it or not, all the soldiers have been ordered to inflict non-lethal damage, but if they can't help it, they are to defend themselves. Understand? If you come across any fights, tell them I sent you. My name is Arryn."

He nodded. "Thank you. You should know that five hundred of Zuri's men went north with him."

Her eyes widened. "*What?*"

"Zuri. He left before we did. They were all on horses and rode through the desert as fast as they could to make it north in time. The plan was to send someone to watch the city for the queen and her army to leave. Once they did..."

Arryn's shoulders fell. "Jadid would be left with minimal protection, and he'd be able to sack the city."

He nodded again.

"Go. Save as many good men as you can," she ordered. "I have to alert the queen. Thank you for your help."

Before he could say anything else, Snow leapt over the wall of men and landed a few feet away, having sensed her druid's distress. The tiger was covered in blood, but that didn't stop Arryn from climbing on her back.

"We have to find the queen," Arryn said.

She erected a barrier around them as Snow charged through the fighting men. To her surprise, several of Zuri's men fought others. It seemed the tide was slowly turning. The soldiers had been successful in changing the minds of at least a few.

When Arryn and Snow charged into a large, wide-open area, she saw Asim and her daughters fighting several magicians. Arryn watched in fascination as the queen stomped, the ground shaking even under Arryn. She split her hands apart, and the sand parted as it swallowed the three men she battled up to the chest, their arms and legs immobilized.

When another man charged her, she leapt, flipping over once before landing gracefully on her feet. As the man turned, she kicked him hard in the chest, sending him back more than ten feet.

"Let's go," Arryn said, and Snow obeyed.

"What is it?" Asim asked as Arryn rode up.

"It's Zuri. I turned one of his men, and he said five hundred of their men went north with Zuri. They waited outside the city for us to move out."

The queen's eyes widened. "We're a full day out! What the hell do we do?"

Her face contorted in rage as a man in black ran toward her. She took several quick steps forward, and Arryn could feel the hate rolling off her. She sure as hell wouldn't want to be on her bad side right then. The man swung, and Asim caught his fist in one hand while using the heel of the other to snap his elbow backward.

He screamed as she twisted it behind his back, dropping him on the ground before she grabbed his head and jerked, ending him.

When the queen turned, Arryn stared at her with wide eyes. "What?" Asim barked.

Arryn held up both hands. "Nothing. I saw nothing."

Asim's breaths came fast as fear and adrenaline flooded

through her. "Those in black are Zuri's men. They've all been dressed the same, and they're all just as filthy as the next."

"I just took on four of them, and you're not wrong." She paused as Bast and Cleo ran up. She gave her daughters a brief smile before turning back to Arryn. "What do we do?"

"We need to go back quickly. Over a day away, there's not much we can do to stop whatever's happening right now, but we *can* end his future reign of terror."

"What's happening?" Cleo asked, and Arryn filled them in.

"We'll go with you," Bast said. "We can't let Jadid fall."

Arryn shook her head. "You also can't let this army overtake yours. They outnumber us."

"So, what?" Cleo asked sarcastically. "You're going to run back to the city and take on all five hundred of Zuri's men alone?"

She shook her head. "There won't be that many by the time I get there because the remaining Guard, as well as any well-trained civilians, will have taken out the majority." Anger that she'd had to say that overwhelmed her. "Do we have anyone capable of teleportation?"

"I'm unsure. It's possible, but it would be hard to find. Unfortunately, you might be more likely to find that among Zuri's men since they aren't trained in Kemetian magic. Far outside the city, people connect with whatever suits them best," Asim said.

Arryn's eyes flashed white as she reached out to the man who turned to their side. She found him and connected easily. *Do you or anyone you've managed to pull back to the queen's side have teleportation abilities?* she sent.

Yes. A few do. I don't have any magic, he quickly responded. She could see flashes of him fighting alongside a royal soldier.

Send them north of the battle. I need their help to get to the city.

CHAPTER TWENTY-SIX

Corrine and Amara sat and waited for what felt like forever, watching a large battle take place in front of them while doing nothing.

"Is this what it's always like?" Amara asked.

Corrine nodded. "For the most part. I know I'm strong enough to take care of myself, but I also know this is a bit too much. We'll be the most help when people need healing or there isn't a large group."

"Like that one over there?" Amara asked. "Those guards are outnumbered."

"Shit," Corrine said, debating what to do. If they didn't intervene, the group of four queen's soldiers would be taken down. If she did, she could risk getting hurt. "Let's go."

"Seriously?" Amara asked. "Will Arryn kick our asses?"

Corrine shrugged. "Only if we wind up dead. Trust me, you *don't* want to piss her off."

Dante responded to Corrine's directions and rushed toward the fight. She jumped off him at the last minute, and Amara did the same from the back of her horse. The horse turned and ran back while Dante leapt close to the larger fight to keep anyone else from joining in.

Corrine's eyes flashed blue as she felt power surge through her body. "Here we go. Time to see what I can do."

When the physical magic users attempted to leave the battlefield, several of Zuri's men attacked them, causing another fight. Arryn and the others rushed forward, but she hesitated, taking a hard punch to the face as a result.

She grunted as she jabbed the thick man in his soft belly. He swung again, but he missed when she ducked.

"Everything okay?" Cleo called.

"It's..." she rose and punched the man hard in the face, knocking him off-balance, "Corrine," she forced out. "Dante says she's rushing into battle."

"Go!" Asim called. "We'll get the men out. Go to the girls."

Arryn climbed onto the tiger's back again and ran toward Corrine. It didn't take long to find the girls, and when her eyes locked onto Corrine, they widened as her jaw fell open.

Corrine's eyes flashed blue as she rushed into battle. The girl leapt and mule-kicked a man in the back hard enough that he flew several feet. She landed flat on her back in the soft sand and rolled out of the way as a large man stomped at her.

Her hand whipped up and a ball of sand hit him in the face, then she kicked out, breaking his knee. When he fell, she punched him in the head and knocked him out.

Amara thrust her hands out, telekinetic energy throwing a man back as he ran toward Corrine. Arryn watched in amazement as Corrine charged forward, planting her foot on his leg before flipping backward and kicking him under the chin. He landed on his back, and Amara slugged him hard in the face to incapacitate him.

Dante took out several men trying to run toward Corrine. She trusted him, so she paid no attention to those men as she continued to go for the group fighting the Kemetian soldiers. Arryn thought about interfering, but the soldiers were holding their own, and the girl was kicking ass. The druid wanted to see what she was capable of.

Two men turned away from the other soldiers and ran toward her. She did several back handsprings before landing on one knee in the sand. As she stood, sandy whips rose with her hands. She smiled as she began to lash out with her arms and the sandy whips tore her opponents' skin.

One dodged an attack from one of her whips, only for her to swing the second, wrapping it around his neck and throwing him far from her. The other man stopped in his tracks and clutched his chest before falling to the ground. The second he was down, Arryn saw Amara's eyes return to normal.

She'd used the death touch, but only enough to weaken the man charging for Corrine. While Arryn didn't like that she'd used it at all, she'd stopped herself and had done it to protect Corrine. She made a mental note to talk to Cathillian about it later.

The soldiers took down the final few and turned to the girls. Arryn nudged Snow forward as they approached the heroines of the day.

"Thank you," one of the soldiers said. He was wounded in several places and limping.

Corrine's eyes flashed neon-green as she lifted a hand and healed the small group of men just enough to be able to stand upright again. "You're welcome," she said with a big smile.

Arryn almost laughed. Her daughter had been a total badass, but she still had that cheesy, childlike grin. It made her happy to see it.

"What are you doing here?" Corrine asked.

"Dante warned me you were heading into battle. I came to help." Arryn looked around. "But I see you didn't need it."

"See? I'm not so bad after all, huh?"

Arryn shook her head, still smiling. "Not even a little."

Corrine turned to Dante. "You're a rat, not a cat."

The tiger grumbled in response.

"I have to go back to Jadid, and I think you should both come with me," Arryn said.

Both girls looked offended. "What? Retreat? The battle isn't over yet!" Corrine said.

"No, you don't understand. Zuri took a lot of men north early. He's attacking the city, more than likely right this second." She turned to Amara. "If you want the revenge you seek, you need to go back with me."

"I'm going," she said without hesitation.

Corrine nodded. "If he's there now, a lot of people will be in bad shape. I'm coming too."

"Arryn," Bast called behind her.

She turned to see fifteen men running alongside Amon, the princesses, the queen, and a few Queen's Guard who had refused to let her go alone.

"These are the physical magic users you requested," Asim said.

Arryn smiled. "Just in time. Who's ready to go back to Jadid and reclaim it in the name of the queen?"

By the time Asim and the others got the physical magicians free, hundreds of men in the opposing army had discovered the truth and began to turn on the others, doing their best to save as many as possible. Zuri's numbers were dwindling fast, but that didn't matter. It had never mattered to him. His goal had always been the city, and he'd used all those people as a distraction to get what he wanted.

Though it pained her to say it, Talia had taught Arryn a very big lesson in teamwork when it came to physical magic. The more, the merrier, and power could be shared when there was a common goal.

With sixteen people able to teleport, they could transport themselves, Arryn, the girls, Amon, and the tigers longer distances. They would have to conserve their energy by making small jumps, but Jadid was much closer to where they started than the Frozen North had been to Arcadia when Talia and fewer people had transported Arryn to the top of the mountains.

After four jumps, they reached the city. While no one felt their best, they weren't drained, and that had been the point. When they arrived, Arryn was prepared to see the city on fire, people screaming, and the world in chaos. What she found was nothing shy of mind-blowing.

The sky was dark, and lightning webbed across it. A few hundred feet away, Arryn saw a large red-skinned figure. It was feminine in nature, but she couldn't sense anything *bad* about it.

"Is that..." Amon started. His eyes flashed steel gray-blue, and he shook his head. "I don't know what that is, but it's not dark. I don't understand. It *has* to be one of those monsters. Red skin. Horns."

Arryn nodded. "I don't sense anything bad either."

"Do you plan to join me in saving the city, or are you going to sit and watch the show?" a masculine voice said in her mind.

She looked at Amon, but he shook his head. "That wasn't me."

Arryn stepped forward. "Whoever it was is on our side. If that monster isn't fighting against us, we have no reason to be afraid. Let's go."

Snow knelt to allow Arryn to mount with less effort, and Dante did the same so Corrine and Amara could climb onto his back. They all ran forward, and Arryn pulled her bow from her back.

With this group, she didn't have to worry about anyone with a good conscience. She could see the darkness in their hearts as she got closer, and she let the arrows fly. She nocked and loosed one arrow after another as she rode in large circles.

Her eyes wandered to the red-skinned figure, and she realized it, or rather she, didn't look like a monster. She was just over six feet tall, with a long, lean, curvy body. She thwarted Zuri's men with little effort. As she slammed another to the ground, stepping on his chest, her eyes wandered to Arryn.

Focus! the masculine voice hissed in her mind.

Arryn heard the scream of a child, and she turned to see a woman cut down as she tried to flee with her toddler in her arms.

"Corrine!" Arryn shouted as she dismounted from Snow.

The younger druid slid to a stop by Arryn's side, her hands flying out in front of her as her eyes turned neon-green. As Corrine focused on healing the mother and possibly the child, Arryn ran toward the group of men who'd injured them.

Arryn smiled as they lunged at her. "That was a *big* fucking mistake. I'm back on solid ground now, bitches."

Her eyes flashed green, and vines burst through the ground. One wrapped around her first target, lifting him into the air before slamming him to the ground and snapping his neck. She then reached into the sky, feeling the moisture lingering in it from it evaporation off the great river.

She pulled her hands down and ice spikes formed. Flinging her arms outward, she took out the other two. A man grabbed her from behind, and she kicked upward with incredible flexibility, striking him in the face. He stumbled back, and she thrust a hand out. He flew several feet back and landed hard on the ground, where Corrine quickly ended him.

Though Arryn didn't like it, his wasn't the first life Corrine had taken, and Arryn had learned not to underestimate her.

Stop worrying about the girl. She's doing fine. Behind you.

She turned as the voice warned her, and she saw a wall of men headed her way. Thunder cracked overhead again, and she decided to use the resources she had available to her. She lifted her hand to the sky as if reaching for something, and when she yanked down, a lightning bolt struck the ground, throwing men in different directions.

Interesting, the voice said in her mind, but she ignored it.

Thanks for the commentary and the warnings, but if you're not going to show your face, stay the fuck out of my head. I don't like intruders I don't know, she sent back.

If you had a sufficient mental barrier and weren't so distracted, I wouldn't have to keep intervening—Arryn of the Dark Forest.

That caught her off-guard, but she realized he had probably picked that up from her mind. Shaking it off, she put her arms straight out and called the rain. It began to pour all around her, and as the remaining fighters grew closer, she froze it into thousands of tiny balls.

"You shouldn't have come for Jadid," she said. "Please accept my welcome gift."

She thrust her hands forward and the projectiles soared through the air, piercing dozens of men. She stumbled back and realized she'd used far too much energy. The ice balls hadn't cut through even half of them, and she still needed to get to Zuri.

Turning, she saw Amon fighting with several men. He took on five at once. It didn't take much for her to realize he'd been very humble when speaking about his skills earlier. As more approached, a giant portal ripped open directly behind him.

Fear took her until she realized it was an illusion Amon had pulled from the minds of his enemies. He sent imaginary beasts chasing others down as he continued to fight. It almost made her laugh to see it.

The leader and several of his men are inside the city. One of the children has gone for him.

"Shit," Arryn said out loud.

As she ran forward, she caught sight of Corrine battling two men. It didn't take much for her to win while using Kemetian magic. She finished them and caught up to Arryn. The younger druid was about to say something when her eyes widened, and her finger pointed.

Turning, Arryn saw an old man with a staff raised high in the air. She felt a familiar tingle and watched from a safe distance as lightning shot down, taking out several men at once. He was a nature-magic user.

Then the man turned and thrust his staff outward, a blast of energy sending a group of men backward as the other physical magicians helped. *He uses physical magic, too?*

GO! the voice shouted in her mind, but she froze for a second when she saw his blood-red eyes staring into hers across what had become a battlefield.

She nodded once before heading into the city. "Corrine! Come with me. Amara went after Zuri alone."

They rushed in, working side by side to fight off Zuri's men when they came at them. Zuri had staggered his troops through the city, so it was relatively easy with them working together.

"I don't have much power left," Arryn said. "But don't heal me. Save it. We have no idea what we'll find."

The tigers roared as they took men down and came to their humans' sides. Each druid climbed onto her mount and rode toward the pyramid palace. As they passed Zuri's men along the way, Arryn shot as many as she could with her bow. The remaining soldiers continued to fight, and she prayed there were enough of them to make a difference.

As they approached the steps of the palace, she saw Zuri sitting at the top with ten men at the base in a straight line. Amara was in front of them, her hands in the air. One of the men grabbed her and dragged her up the stairs.

"Don't fucking hurt her," Arryn growled, both tigers loosing growls of their own.

"Oh, I'm not going to hurt her. I'm going to kill her. I doubt there will be much pain involved in what I have planned."

Arryn opened her senses, but she felt no fear coming from Amara. She wondered if this had been the girl's plan all along. Arryn looked down to hide her white eyes as she reached out.

Was this your plan? Arryn sent.

I'm fine. Don't be scared for me. I'm exactly where I need to be, but you should leave.

I can't. I won't leave until I know you're safe, Arryn replied.

Amara groaned, and Arryn looked up, her white eyes on display. She saw a knife at Amara's throat, but the girl still felt no fear.

"What type of magician are you?" Zuri asked.

Arryn looked up at him. "One that's far too strong for you."

You sure about this? Arryn sent to Amara.

Hell, yes. When I give you the signal, shield yourself and Corrine.

Arryn's eyes widened as she thought through the implications. What did she have planned? Was it powerful enough to hurt them?

Zuri laughed. "Women. You're all the same. You run your mouths all day long and expect to be taken seriously when you're this weak." He tightened his grip on Amara.

A loud laugh escaped Arryn. "Oh, that's hilarious. You can't even *begin* to understand the fatal mistake you've made."

"Yeah? What was that, sweetheart?"

Now. I'm ready now! Amara shouted through the link.

"You made an enemy out of *her*," she said, nodding toward Amara.

The girl's eyes flashed gray with green around the edges, and Arryn formed a shield around herself, Corrine, and the tigers. She watched in horrified amazement as Amara's hands thrust outward. She felt the energy take all eleven men as her death touch grew. The power slammed into Arryn's barrier, and she realized that had she not barricaded them as Amara had warned, it would have touched her, too.

The men choked and gasped for air as blood poured from

their noses. Zuri's hands fell away from Amara as he dropped to his knees, and she turned and looked him in the eyes as he stared into hers.

"I told you I'd find a way," she said as his head hit the ground. "I told you I'd get revenge for the evil you brought. No one deserves what you did, and I'm going to make damn sure you never hurt anyone like that again."

He gasped for air, but she clenched her fists, every one of the men dying on the ground.

"Very interesting indeed," the masculine voice Arryn had heard in her head said from behind her.

She whipped her head around to see a tall man standing next to the red woman, each of them wrapped in a barrier just as she and Corrine were. Arryn felt around to make sure Amara's power had dissipated before she let down her shield and dismounted. She walked up to the man and looked into his red eyes as they faded to normal.

As she studied him, she realized she'd never seen him before, but there was something familiar about him. "Who *are* you?" she asked.

He smiled as he looked down at her, stroking his long beard. "I was hoping I'd get to meet you, though I must say you could use some work."

She growled at him, offended. "Excuse me? I need some work?"

He nodded. "Indeed. You're incredibly powerful, but you have no idea how to tap into it. You're holding back. You don't access all your powers at once, you switch between them. Hmm. Yes, you definitely need some work, but we can do that before the next battle."

"Listen, old man, I don't know who you are—"

He waved his staff and his free hand in the air. "Ah, yes. Forgive me. My name's Ezekiel, though I'd wager where you come from, you might know me as the Founder."

EPILOGUE

It took the queen's army nearly a full day to return, but when they did, the city was on its way to being secure. Arryn took control in the queen's stead and gathered groups of people to help remove the bodies.

She was happy to see that most of the soldiers returned with the queen, but she was surprised to see the monarch return with so many of the men who fought for Zuri. Mistaken or not, they'd still fought against her.

"It's been a long few days," Asim had said. "They have reunited with their families and are welcome to stay in neighboring towns, though they will help build more homes."

When Cathillian walked through the gates, Arryn wrapped her arms around him and kissed him. "You won't fucking believe what happened!"

He laughed. "With you, I never can."

Once there was a clear path to the palace, everyone met under the shelter house, though the only food available was fruit and bread. No one complained as they sat down to eat and discuss the next steps.

"I'm exhausted, and I'd really love to get this over with," Asim said. "No offense, Arryn. I'm sure this is important, but we need sleep."

The druid laughed. "Trust me, I know that more than most. I'm surprised I didn't pass out this time. I usually do."

"That's because you held back and let an old man do the work for you," Ezekiel said from behind her.

Everyone stiffened as he and the red-skinned woman walked up. Arryn rolled her eyes and shook her head. She barely knew the man, and already he was on her ass. She couldn't wait to see what torture was in store for her when they began training. As she opened her mouth to speak, Cathillian's shock wore off enough for him to say, "Holy shit."

"Uh, Arryn?" Asim asked, pointing.

"That's...that's the Founder," Cathillian said, interrupting.

Arryn nodded. "Yes. Everyone, I'd like you to meet Ezekiel, the Founder. And this is Lilith."

"Hello," Lilith said. "I understand that given what all you have heard or seen with an open Rift south of here, my appearance might be shocking. I assure you, I am here to help."

"And we have a lot of work to do," Ezekiel said. "As you know well, war is coming, and we must prepare. Arryn and I have a lot of work to do."

"What kind of work?" Bast asked. "Reinforcing Jadid? Training? If it's training, I'm in. It's not every day you get to meet the Founder." She bowed her head in respect. "I'm a fast learner."

Arryn sighed. "Definitely training. I've been off lately, and it's time I got myself back together. Ezekiel is going to help me do that. After all, he's the one who trained Hannah, and she's been kicking ass all over the world. So, as much as it's going to be a pain in my ass, I'm grateful for it. We have a world to save."

Ezekiel nodded. "Yes, we do. This isn't the first Rift, and it surely won't be the last." He turned to Arryn. "I already trained one Hannah. It looks like I get to suffer through another one who is just as quick-witted. I assure you that this will be just as much a pain in *my* ass."

She smiled. "Well, I *do* try."

FINIS

AUTHOR NOTES - CANDY CRUM

JUNE 7, 2020

WOW! I honestly can't believe it's been two years already! What a wild two years it's been. So many growths, setbacks, lessons learned, and more!

I turned thirty-five in April (or—as I like to call it—my 7th Annual 29th birthday haha!). I always imagined that would be super scary for me, but honestly, I was happy about it! Instead of marking me getting older, it marked my achievements. Over the last year, I've worked super hard to get my life exactly where I want it, and I'm excited to say, it's there.

Because of that positivity, when I write, it's SO much easier. It's back to being my work *and* my hobby. If I go a day without writing or creating something, I feel like I'm going stir crazy! Writing 3,000 words or more in a couple to few short hours now isn't difficult at all, and OH I missed that! The one thing I've learned most over the last two years is that stress is the thief of joy.

Other than that lesson, something that has stayed consistent throughout everything is all of you showing support (especially when I had so many health issues – thank you more than you'll ever know!) and also the friendships I've made within LMBPN.

The employees, the writers, and the readers. It's a family, and I enjoy being a part of it.

With that being said, I'm encroaching on super scary territory! This is book EIGHT! There are only... *nine* books in this core series! You can't see it, but I'm mentally projecting a big ol' shocked face right now. That's crazy! Only one book left!

Now, don't get too worried. I'm going to close the series properly, but it'll be left off in a way that we can pick up in case Arryn decides to get into some shenanigans in the future. I honestly don't think I can ever leave her entirely. That is truly a sad thought!

I'm excited to say my youngest (who is TWELVE NOW—oh my goodness) is working more on an outline for his own book. I love that he wants to write, and I plan to help him in every way. This path was totally his decision—but I *do* think it has a lot to do with me. He's definitely mama's boy, and I love that so much.

He has lots of ideas, and we're working on how to outline and process them so he can write them. He still has a hard time with dedication. He's twelve, though, so I totally understand! I wanted to be an author at his age, and I was the same way. I didn't actually start writing until I was in my mid-twenties. So, we'll get him there if he decides to stick with it! I'm SO proud of him. <3

Another big accomplishment in our house is that I've almost gotten my oldest (fourteen) to stop telling *verbal* stories.

Now, before anyone thinks "CANDY! What a horrible thing to do!" please just hear me out.

This kid... When he TELLS me these stories he comes up with, these monsters he designs (and he draws *every* *single* *one*), the names he comes up with, and the MASSIVE backstories for his characters, I get *so* worked up because I'm thinking, "This kid is a literal storytelling genius, and he won't write any of it down! He's going to forget it at some point, and it'll be lost!"

He's fourteen, and his stories blow me away. His brother and I are both creative, but we have to work at it. Brandon (my oldest), it just comes natural to him. He's more like his dad. His mind has always been a wild and crazy place. One of my *favorite* characters of his is named Matilda, and every time he tells me about her, I think, "Michael would love her."

It's all very sci-fi and has incredibly powerful imagery. He wants to design video games, and that's why he doesn't 'write.' But I told him if he wrote all this stuff down, even just as short stories that were roughly written in a notebook, and kept them for later, he can guarantee he'll never forget. He'll always have them.

Now, he's starting to talk about writing actual books and using it for later to turn into video games or comics. Because of that, he's starting to read. That's something he's never done, which is *wild* to me because he's so good at storytelling. I'm hoping he continues to read and learns more about how to put a story together. So, if he continues down that path, I'll totally let you know. You'll definitely want to read those.

Thank you everyone for sticking with me and supporting me through everything. You are all the absolute best, and I can't wait for all of you to see what's next! I just turned in a sample for a new fantasy series I'm working on called, "The Mortiferian." Unsure yet who will be publishing it, but I'll definitely keep you updated on that and also on The Feisty Druid finale, "Damn the Rift." I've already written a lot of the outline, and I'm starting it soon.

I hope everyone stays safe and happy, and I can't wait to see you on the next one!

The joy of creatives is twice as much when your own children share your passion!

So, in our family, we have three guys, and two of them are professional authors, and one has written fanfic. I'm proud of all three, and sometimes I just have to realize that while they can all write, they might not WANT to write.

Because of that, I now understand how parents might accidentally push their children down a path they don't want to go.

When a parent is pushy, doesn't mean their parenting is horrible. It can mean we don't understand how our children *can't possibly* love what we enjoy when we see they have the talent to be awesome at whatever it is.

In Candy's author notes, it is apparent she doesn't have that challenge in her life, and that is fantastic. Both her boys are showing engagement and interest. I completely understand her oldest wanting to go into video games and desire their advocation to become their vocation.

(I'm secretly hoping my guys all become world-wide bestselling authors and we create an author-family synonymous with writing like the Kennedys or the Bushes in politics, but I keep that to myself.

And apparently now with all of you, too.)

That hyperbolic fantasy aside, it brings a smile to my face when others get a chance to share their passion with family members.

I have a niece who might want to ask Uncle Mike about what he does for a living, and I'm looking forward to that discussion, too.

Who knows, maybe "Anderle" will become a surname well-known to readers over the next decade or two?

I would smile if maybe in the future, there is another collaboration, but this time it isn't Candy Crum and Michael Anderle. Nope, the collaborators are between our children, or our nieces / nephews etc.

I think I'll go find a Coke and drink to that!

Diary Entry Saturday, June 6, 2020 to Friday, June 12, 2020

Las Vegas is slowly opening from the Covid shutdown.

It is interesting what is going on here in Las Vegas as the city slowly opens back up (I live on the Strip, so I don't know what is going on downtown.) I have been to the Venetian / Palazzo Hotels/Casinos on Thursday night and to Gold Coast on Friday night.

Specifically, I wanted the chicken wrap with spicy sauce in the Grand Lux and Chinese food at Ping Pang Pong in Gold Coast.

It was *delicious*.

While I did gamble on Thursday night, it just wasn't the same as I remember back before the Pandemic shut all doors. Back then, everything was either a party, the late-night party, or the people leaving the party and more flying in to start that next night's party.

Now, I'm waiting to see if the folks from California drive here or what happens if they don't. Only a few hotels are open at the moment, and even the restaurants inside the open hotels are occasionally not open for business (or if open, they don't have the same operating hours as before.)

It's really weird.

But I'm thankful it IS happening.

I was talking w/ fellow author Craig Martelle driving to breakfast Wednesday, and I happened to be driving next to the airport and saw one jet land while another was taking off. I then looked around the runways and noticed about five jets lining up, waiting to take off.

My jaw almost dropped.

I hadn't seen jets (more than one) on the tarmac in over two months. The airport had become almost like a ghost town. I remember one night last year counting seven jets lining up, their landing lights trailing off into the sky to land, and recently I couldn't see seven jets at all unless you count a few parked somewhere.

Covid-19 has hurt the planet in so many ways. From the obvious of lives taken early to families' savings wiped out, to pesticides and machinery not able to get to locations for the swarm of billions of locusts rampaging across east Africa and India.

If I had put all of this into a story, I think more than one reader might have told me I had placed too many challenges in the mix, and they thought 'C'mon! Epidemics, swarms, floods, *and* famine? Get real, Michael!'

Real life has hit us all.

And yet, humans fight back. We fight back for all of the right reasons. Sometimes it's amongst ourselves, sometimes against the insect population and sometimes against contagions.

I know that a couple of planes crossing a lonely tarmac in Las Vegas isn't the same kind of sign as a beautiful flower amongst a destroyed landscape, but for me personally, it was a small sign that we as a world are getting back on our feet.

May you find your own flower as we rise up out of a completely horrible first half of 2020.

Ad Aeternitatem,

Michael Anderle

BOOKS BY CANDY CRUM

TALES OF THE FEISTY DRUID
with Michael Anderle

The Arcadian Druid (01) - The Undying Illusionist (02) - The Frozen Wasteland (03) - The Deceiver (04) - The Lost (05) - The Damned (06) Into The Maelstrom (07) Legends Of The Ancients (08)

THE THERIAN CHRONICLES
with Amanda Browning

The Dark Professor (1) The Therian Prince (2)

Reclaiming The Shadow Realm

The Usurper (1) Darkness Rising (2) Shadow Born (3)

Stand-Alone Novels

Stranger Than Fiction

BOOKS BY MICHAEL ANDERLE

For a complete list of books by Michael Anderle, please visit

www.lmbpn.com/ma-books/

All LMBPN Audiobooks are Available at Audible.com and iTunes. For a complete list of audiobooks visit:

www.lmbpn.com/audible

CONNECT WITH THE AUTHORS

To see ALL of Candy's different books check out her website below

Website:
http://www.candycrumbooks.com

Facebook
https://www.facebook.com/groups/thecandyshopgroup/

Michael Anderle Social

Website:
http://www.lmbpn.com

Email List:
http://lmbpn.com/email/

www.ingramcontent.com/pod-product-compliance
Lightning Source LLC
Chambersburg PA
CBHW050257110726
47898CB00007B/2450